PAINT IT BLACK

A
J.D HAWKINS MYSTERY

Books by Rodman Philbrick

Slow Dancer
Brothers and Sinners

J.D. Hawkins Mystery Series
Shadow Kills
Ice for the Eskimo
Paint it Black
Walk On the Water

T.D. Stash Mystery Series
The Neon Flamingo
The Crystal Blue Persuasion
Tough Enough

PAINT
IT
BLACK

Rodman Philbrick

SPEAKING VOLUMES, LLC

NAPLES, FLORIDA

2013

Paint it Black

ISBN 978-1-61232-843-0

For all you secret sharers, adrift in your books, dream on.

CHAPTER ONE

HE CAME AROUND THE CORNER THE WAY they said he would, running flat out. A young, blond-haired cop who'd lost his hat and his gun. Not bothering, in his haste, to check the sidewalk for cracks. Just picking them up and putting them down as if his life depended on it.

I was in the squad car, waiting at the intersection of Exeter and Beacon Street. The kid with the yellow hair and the blurred feet was supposed to be my partner. I had no idea what had got into him—or more to the point, how he'd lost his lid and his sidearm. Given a few moments, I'd have figured it out. But we didn't have a few moments. I had a couple of heartbeats more than he did, but in the end it didn't matter, it all went down so fast.

The kid got to the car. He grabbed the door handle just as I fumbled and released the lock. Before he could open the door a red hole appeared in his neck. The side window exploded. The bits of exploded window were all over my lap. The kid appeared to be staring at the broken glass as blood pulsed from his wound. The shattered glass looked like rock salt, or uncut diamonds. Maybe he took that image with him as he died.

The man who shot my partner was Smilin' Stan Seigel, who'd never smiled in his life, so far as anyone knew. He sure wasn't smiling when he leaned in through the broken window and put the muzzle of my partner's service revolver between my eyebrows and pulled the trigger.

That was how I died the first time.

"So," I said to Lindy Bangs, the director, "was it okay? Did I die good?"

"You died great, Jack."

"You gonna shoot it again?"

Lindy grinned, snapping a wad of electric pink bubble gum. "You loved it, huh? Sorry, honey, we got it the first take. And a good thing, too. With the special traffic detail and the gunplay, just the one shot cost five, six grand to set up. A low-budget TV movie like this, you don't do a second take unless you damn well need it."

The young actor who had portrayed my partner got to his feet and flashed a thumbs-up. Stage blood continued to pulse from the fake wound on his neck, which got a few laughs from the film crew. Someone brought my wheelchair alongside the cruiser and I managed to make the transfer without requiring assistance.

That was it. My brief career as a movie actor was over. I hadn't blown any lines because it was a nonspeaking part. All that had been required of me was a look of dumb surprise upon being shot in the head with a wad of sticky red gelatin.

No problem. Looking dumb and surprised is one of my main strengths. That's how I looked, fifteen minutes later, when Megan Drew jogged onto the set and announced that my old pal Lieutenant Detective Tim Sullivan had been blown up in his car.

Meg had been at work when she got the call. As there had been no cabs immediately available, and as the movie location was only about ten blocks from the Beacon Hill offices of Standish House Publishing, Meg had jogged all the way there. One of the unplanned benefits of wearing Nikes to work is the ability to make a run for it when an emergency requires an immediate response.

"He's been taken to Beth Israel," Meg said, getting her breath back.

"So he's still alive?"

She shrugged helplessly. "All Marilyn said was, he's been rushed to the nearest hospital. I assume they'd take him to a hospital no matter what. Even if he was dead at the scene. Isn't that what they do?"

"Blown up," I said. "Jesus. What happened?"

"Get your van, Jack. Let's get over there."

I drove. Not because my nerves were steadier than Meg's, but because the van is set up to accommodate a paraplegic behind the wheel. While we inched through the traffic in Kenmore Square, Meg explained that Marilyn, Sully's secretary at the Homicide Unit, had first tried to phone me at home, then tried Megan's work number. The information about Sully had come through the Turret, the police radio headquarters.

"I got the idea she really didn't know the details," Meg said. "You know Marilyn, right? The iron maiden. She said—let me think—she said, 'Sully's car has been blown up in his driveway. They've taken him to Beth Israel. I thought you'd want to know, before you heard it elsewhere.'"

"That's all?"

"You've got the light, Jack."

I hit the hand lever and goosed through the intersection onto Brookline Avenue, thinking it was a good thing the Red Sox were on a September road trip, or the Kenmore Square area would have been in gridlock.

Meg said, "Yeah, poor Marilyn sounded really shook up. She loves the guy, you know?"

I'd never really thought about it. Tim Sullivan was a lifelong bachelor of ascetic inclination, a remarkably astute detective whose only serious relationship was with his work. His longtime secretary, on the other hand, was happily married to a plumbing contractor. Knowing the two of them, an office romance was out of the question. But if any woman loved Sully, Marilyn did, in her stubborn way.

As I began scanning the area around the Beth Israel complex for a place to double park, the thing that struck me as weird was the part about Sully's car being blown up in his driveway. Had he been shot in the line of duty I'd have been shocked but not terribly surprised. Getting shot can happen to a cop. It can happen to a civilian working in the department, as I'd found out the hard way. But getting blown up was, in my book, confined to Mafia stool pigeons or enemies of the Irish Republican Army, neither of which category included Tim Sullivan.

Ordinarily I choose not to park in the slots for the handicapped, leaving them for the genuinely infirm. This time I made an exception, and we headed up the sidewalk to the emergency entrance. Meg had to break into a jog to keep up with my wheels.

Larry Sheehan, who worked under Sully at Homicide, was in the corridor, blowing smoke at the admitting nurse.

"Lady," he was saying, "these are Lucky Strikes,

okay? If I gave a shit about your nonsmoking regs, I'd be smoking Kools or some other filter job, but I *don't* give a shit about your nonsmoking regs, okay?"

"What does Lucky Strike have to do with it?" the nurse demanded.

Larry held up the pack. "Read the fine print, lady. Lucky Strike means fuck the regs. So get out of my face before I bust you for interfering with an officer of the law."

I had to smile at the inimitable Sheehan logic. The nurse, seeing she was up against a confirmed delinquent, returned to her desk and picked up the phone. Dealing with Sergeant Detective Lawrence Sheehan tends to inspire efforts to contact a higher authority, in this case the hospital security force, which prudently failed to respond.

Sheehan spotted us and started giving me a hard time. With him, it's pure instinct.

"Hey," he said, "I musta called Marilyn a half hour ago, right after I heard. It takes you thirty minutes to go two miles?"

I ignored the jibe and asked, "How is he, Larry? What happened?"

"All they'll tell me," he said, "he was alive when they brung him in. They got him in surgery right now. Naturally I tried to get in there, make sure they know they've got a very important person, they better not mess around. They locked the goddamn door on me, that's what they did. The bastards."

Larry Sheehan is a tough little guy with a duck's ass haircut combed straight back from a pale, wrinkled forehead, a permanent squint, and a way of talking that makes it sound like he's got rocks in his mouth. The twang is from Chelsea, where he was born and will probably die, if he lives long enough to retire. He doesn't have much use for me for several reasons, the most important being that I had had the effrontery to attend Boston Latin (in his words a "fag elite" school) and because I sued the Boston Police Department for a lot of money, and won. Brad Dorsey, the cop who accidentally put a bullet in my spine, was a friend of Sheehan's once upon a time, and the code of the Chelsea streets is that you never forget a friend, or comfort his enemy.

Despite our many differences, we did have a few things in common. One of them was Tim Sullivan, who'd stood up for me when everyone else in the department considered me a disgrace, and who had similarly defended Sheehan when the cop bureaucracy wanted him off the force.

"They told you he was alive, but that's all?"

"It's like a state secret, you know? I say, is the guy breathing on his own, is he conscious, what? All I get is the runaround. 'Wait for doctor,' you know?"

I knew all about waiting for doctor. Just being inside a hospital brought into sharp focus the memory of my legs being poked with needles, and the resulting sensation of dread when I did not feel the pain.

Members of the department began to drift in. Nick Gallo, the debonair detective who'd worked for Sully before transferring to the mayor's staff. Liam "The Weasel" Delaney, the commissioner's deputy. Stan Staskowski, who ran the firing range. None of them close friends, because Sully wasn't the kind of guy who had close friends, but each loyal in his own way.

"This ain't no death watch," Sheehan announced, lighting up another Lucky with hands that trembled slightly. "Just don't get no ideas like that. He's gonna be okay."

"Is that what the doctors said?" Gallo wanted to know. "Sully's gonna make it?"

Sheehan glowered, puffing hard on the cigarette. "He's gonna be okay, so just leave it at that. I don't want no argument from nobody."

Nobody argued. Gallo and Staskowski conferred in whispers. Delaney wrote things down in his little blue notebook, just to make sure everyone knew he reported to the commissioner. Sheehan wore tread marks in the linoleum.

"Fuckin' bomb," he said. "Can you believe that? Responding officer says the front end of the car ended up across the street, all in pieces."

"Could it have been an accident?" I asked. "Something wrong with the engine?"

Sheehan gave me a look. "Jesus freaking Christ," he said, disgusted. "You ever hear of a car engine going off like a stick of dynamite? No way. Had to be an explosive device."

"Had to be," I agreed.

You don't have to be a physicist to know that time is relative. All you have to do is wait outside an emergency O.R. while a team of trauma specialists work over a friend. Forty minutes went by like the interval of an Ice Age.

When the chief surgeon came out the first thing he did was bum a cigarette from Larry Sheehan. The bloodied doctor grinned, rolling the cigarette between his freshly scrubbed fingers, and I knew that Sully was alive.

"I'll give you the list," the surgeon said, putting out the Lucky after a couple of shallow puffs. "Fourteen shards of glass removed from the lower back and buttocks—shallow cuts, mostly, but there had been considerable bleeding. Six fractured ribs, one of which resulted in a punctured right lung. Good-sized gash to the forehead, required eighteen sutures. Multiple contusions to arms and hands. Possible concussion. The radiologist is setting up a CAT scan now. No swelling of the brain tissues, but we'll monitor vital signs, just in case."

"So he's okay?"

The surgeon chuckled. "'Okay' is not how I would characterize his condition. He's hurting all over, or will be when he regains consciousness. The punctured lung is serious, of course, but not really unusual. The procedure is well established—basically you repair the puncture wound and reinflate the lung."

"Like a flat tire," Sheehan said hopefully.

The surgeon grinned. "Sort of. Anyhow, I foresee no long-term problems regarding lung damage. The major concern is the trauma to the head, and as I said, we'll have to go over the X-rays and monitor his vital signs carefully. There's always a danger with head trauma. Give us twenty-four hours and we'll have a much better picture."

"So he's not out of the woods?"

"Not quite," he said. "Can I bum another smoke?"

"Sure thing, Doc," Sheehan said. "Help yourself."

They let us have a quick peek at the unconscious victim, who lay on a gurney in the recovery room. Sully looked very small and vulnerable. His face was bruised and bandaged and an IV ran into his left forearm.

Sheehan vowed to stay in there with him until he regained consciousness.

"Somebody's gotta make sure they don't mess with the lieutenant," he said in a husky whisper. "I heard where sometimes they put the wrong patient in surgery, start amputating perfectly good limbs and stuff."

The nurse, recognizing an immovable object, ignored Sheehan and chased the rest of us out.

The police reporters were showing up just as we exited the hospital. They headed for Liam Delaney and his blue notebook. Nick Gallo took the opportunity to sidle over as Meg and I headed for the van.

"Helluva thing, huh? You being close to Sully, I thought maybe you'd have a line on what happened."

"Nobody's really close to Tim Sullivan, Nick. You worked for him, you know that. If you're asking me do I know who'd want to kill him, the answer is no."

"Whoa," Gallo said, holding up his well-manicured hands. "Back it up, okay? I'm just making conversation here. I guess a thing like this happens, we all get a little nervous."

"I guess we do," I said, easing up. "So how're you doing, Nick? You like being on the mayor's staff?"

"Hey," he said, "it beats working. Seriously though, how's it going with you? I've, ah, been reading in the paper about that TV movie they're making, based on a book of yours. That must be pretty exciting, huh?"

"Beats working," I said.

Gallo smiled and then shrugged. "I, ah, think it was Sheehan told me you're going to be in it, the movie."

"In just the one scene," I said. "I'm no actor, that's for sure. It's what they call a lollipop, Nick. The idea is to distract the author from the fact that they've changed his script around."

"They can do that?"

I laughed. "Sure they can."

Gallo looked at Megan and cleared his throat, as if uneasy about speaking in her presence. Finally he spit it out. "Jack, old buddy. About this movie. You pull any weight with this television outfit?"

We were coming, I gathered, to the thrust of the conversation. It wasn't a great surprise to learn that Gallo wanted to be in the movie, in some undefined capacity. I'd been getting similar requests from friends and acquaintances since long before filming began. "Look,

Nick, I'm not putting you off," I said, launching into my standard response. "I'd help if I could. The sad fact is the author has almost no influence. Less than the average grip or electrician working on the crew. Less than the hairstylist or the caterer. Any time I express any opinions the director's eyes begin to glaze over."

"That bad, huh?"

I shrugged. "I took the money. Now it's their baby. I knew that when I signed the contract."

"I'm embarrassed for asking."

"Hey," I said, "don't be. Maybe you've got weight of your own to swing. You work for His Honor, and it's his office that grants permits to the film crew. That ought to be worth something."

Gallo nodded sheepishly and started to walk away. He turned back and said, "Helluva thing about Sully, huh?"

"Yeah," I said. "Helluva thing."

She watched the hospital from the street. Men came and went, some in uniform, some not. It didn't matter, she could always tell a cop. The way they skulked together, the brotherhood. One of them was inside now, in the care of doctors.

Him, the one who had lied to God.

She began to pray. As she prayed the Voices came to her. Out of the clouds, out of the sky. A darkness gathered. A hovering of wings.

Take him, she prayed. Make him die.

CHAPTER TWO

ABOUT THE BOOKS AND THE MOVIE. ONCE upon a time I was employed by the Boston Police Department as a technical writer for Informational Services. By day I wrote pamphlets like *Statistical Evidence of Effects of the Bartley-Fox Gun Law.* By night I was in the habit of frequenting police bars, where I collected cop stories, intending to use them in the novels I somehow never found the time to write.

You get the picture. Frustrated novelist who opts for the security of a steady job. Life was a little boring, but fairly pleasant nonetheless. That all changed, one boozy evening, when a psychologically unbalanced vice cop named Brad Dorsey decided to impress his barroom cronies by firing off his service revolver. A bullet ricocheted off the concrete floor, went through the booth where I was sitting, and put me on wheels for life. Finian X. Fitzgerald, the noted barrister, raconteur, and loudmouth (and my good friend) sued the Boston Police Department on my behalf. The money we won bought me a brand-new wheelchair, a custom-equipped van, a Beacon Street apartment, and the time to write.

The books are about Lieutenant Casey of the fictional Boston Homicide Division, and the crimes he investigates. Some people believe the character of Casey is based on Tim Sullivan, who holds the same rank in the real Boston Homicide Unit, and who has similar physical characteristics. I won't debate the point, except to say that having lived with Casey through seven books, I know what makes him tick, whereas Sully remains for me an enigma wrapped in a mystery.

Okay, the movie. The movie is supposed to be based on *Casey and the Black Widow*, the widow being the wife of a black cop shot in the line of duty. It won't surprise you to know that Casey solves the crime. If you want to know how and why (which is the interesting part), read the book—the way things turned out, I can't recommend the movie.

My troubles started the day before filming was to begin. I managed to get my hands on part of the shooting script, which appeared to be radically different from the screenplay I'd written.

"What's going on here?" I said, waving the new title page in the very attractive face of Lindy Bangs, the twenty-seven-year-old director. "Is this a misprint? A typo? What?"

"You gotta understand," she said, "television is demographics. A feature film, they might go with the black widow angle. TV is all about sex appeal."

"So you changed it to *Casey and the Blond Widow*? Is it cynical of me to assume the black cop is no longer black?"

"What can I say?" she said with a don't-blame-me smile. "He's blond, like the wife. We figured on keeping your symmetry in that regard."

You can see the problem. If having a book edited is like dealing with a flinty-eyed schoolmarm who catches every mistake, having a movie made from that book is like watching a mischievous infant tear it apart page by page. An infant with an infuriatingly disarming smile.

As previously mentioned, the irate author had settled for a "lollipop" scene, and decided it was a lot of fun being an actor, especially if all he had to do was look dumb, surprised, and dead, in that order. Megan Drew, to whom I was then engaged, had a different slant on my sudden infatuation with film.

"You're smitten with whatsername with all the red hair and the itsy-bitsy waist."

"Lindy Bangs."

"The perfect name for the likes of her."

"Meg, I am not smitten with Lindy Bangs. I'm mad as hell at her for ruining my script."

That was true enough, as far as it went. What I felt for Lindy Bangs wasn't love, exactly, and I did have strong feelings about seeing Casey, who is supposed to be taciturn and physically slight, transmogrified into a handsome, wisecracking hunk.

"If you don't want to watch them ruin your story," Meg advised, "stay off the set. And if you still intend to marry me on Christmas Eve in Nantucket, I suggest you stop drooling over Ms. Giddy Bang-Bang, or whatever she calls herself."

"Megan Drew," I said, "you're jealous."

"Of her? No way. You want my advice, Jack? Forget about the movie. Forget about the people involved in making it. Forget about everything but writing your next book."

I knew she was right. The trouble was, the movie was being filmed on location in the Back Bay neighborhood where we lived. Megan got away from it—and me—by going to Standish House each weekday morning, where she was now a senior editor specializing in nonfiction projects. I was stuck at home, supposedly working on my next Casey book, where the idea of the movie being made on the streets below, and, yes, the idea of Lindy Bangs, was a constant temptation.

After the bomb went off, though, there were more important things to distract me from work. The first, somewhat maddening piece of the puzzle was supplied by Larry Sheehan, who appeared on my doorstep the morning after Sully was hospitalized.

"I guess you're pretty busy, huh?" he said, hanging back.

"Come on in."

We had coffee in the kitchen. Sheehan had never been inside the apartment before, and I could see him taking it all in. The lowered counters, the controls and appliances near to hand, the various adjustments made to accommodate a man confined to a wheelchair. He was more nervous in my presence than usual, and for just a moment I had the impression he was going to lobby me for a part in the movie. That's where my head was at. He had the movie on his mind, all right, but for a very different reason. It took him a while to get to the point.

"It was the damnedest thing," he said, "talking to Sully as he was coming out of anesthesia. I mean, I never seen the guy take even a drink, and there he was licking his lips and running off at the mouth like a typical junkie. You know, like he was high? Which I guess he kinda was, with all that dope in him."

"What did he say?"

"Weird stuff. Just between you and me," Sheehan leaned forward, as if he expected to be overheard, "the first thing he does, he asks for his mother. Who, God bless her, has been dead five years at least."

14

"Ouch," I said.

"The thing is, somebody on the outside, who didn't know what a tough little hombre Sullivan is, they might get the wrong impression, you know?"

"Larry," I said. "It has nothing to do with toughness or courage, what people say when they're under. When I was in the hospital there was this old guy in the bed next to me. Veteran of the First World War. Decorated for courage under fire. And all the time he was dying, and it took a while, he kept asking for his mother. Just like Sully."

"Yeah, well the lieutenant ain't dyin'."

I left it at that, and asked if he'd mentioned anything about the bomb or the explosion.

"Not exactly. Understand, the lieutenant was wacked out. He was having what they call a stream of conscience, know what I mean?"

"I think I do," I said, keeping a straight face.

"Well," he said. "First it was asking for his mother, where was she, was she okay, stuff like that. Then Sully says, 'Look out, I'm flying.' He musta said that twenty times, over and over."

"Look out, I'm flying?"

"Yeah. I try to calm him down a little, but he doesn't know I'm there. He's off in never-never land. He starts, and this is the weird part, if you know Sully, he starts talking about some bitch."

"A woman?" I said.

"Sure, a woman. Only he calls her a bitch."

"His mother, maybe?"

"Hey, I gotta say I never heard the lieutenant say an unkind word about his mom. Did you?"

"Nope. I don't think I ever heard Sully use the word *bitch*. Except *son of a bitch*. Never in reference to a woman."

Sheehan laughed and drained his coffee cup. "Know what? I get a kick out of the way you talk, Hawkins. 'Never in reference to a woman,' that's like out of a book or something."

"Okay, Larry, I love you, too. Now what about this 'bitch'? She have anything to do with the bomb?"

He shrugged, a gesture that carried up through his eyebrows. "He says, 'I'm not in the movie, you crazy bitch. I'm not in the movie.' Said it over and over, like he was arguing with someone. Then he kept saying 'get off the line, get off the line.' Like, you know, some bitch was on the phone and he was trying to get rid of her."

I said, "Not just a bitch, Larry. A crazy bitch. Crazy enough to try and blow him up, maybe? Is that your idea?"

Sheehan was playing with the coffee cup, spinning the handle. "I dunno," he said, avoiding eye contact. "I thought maybe it had something to do with this movie they're making. That's what he kept saying, 'I'm not in the movie.' You know anything about that, Hawkins? Sully and the movie?"

Tim Sullivan had never, to my knowledge, expressed any interest in the Casey film or any other, for that matter. The normal, everyday conversations that touched on movies or television were always ignored by Sully. He assumed a blank, bored look, as if such frivolities were not worthy of discussion. So I could understand why Sheehan thought it odd that Sully would be raving on the subject.

"Guy never went to a movie in his life, am I right?" Sheehan said. "At least not since I worked with him. Only thing he ever watches on the tube is a ball game, and even then he turns the sound down so low you can hardly hear."

"'I'm not in the movie, you crazy bitch. Get off the line.'"

Sheehan said, "Pretty weird, huh?"

I agreed. But it might not have any more significance than a nightmare someone has while under the influence of a powerful drug. Random words strung together by a fevered mind. The result, perhaps, of a concussion. And yet Sheehan, who I had gradually come to regard as being astute in such matters, thought it important enough to repeat to me.

"You think I know something about this," I said. "*That's* why you're here."

Again the whole-body shrug that started somewhere below the knees and extended to his eyebrows, causing his brow to furrow into a deep V. "Hey, what do I know?" he said. "I figure Sully is trying to tell me something important about a woman, a phone call, and a movie. The movie makes me think of you, naturally, since you're involved with this television thing that's about the lieutenant, right?"

I sighed. "You could look at it that way, I guess. You're not the only person who thinks Casey is based on Tim Sullivan."

"It's what everybody says, Jack."

"Granted. But Sully himself doesn't have anything to do with how I write the books or how they make the movie, and he sure as hell isn't *in* the movie. I shudder to think what he'd say if anybody suggested as much."

"Well," Sheehan said. "Maybe somebody did."

CHAPTER THREE

AFTER SHEEHAN LEFT I WENT TO MY DESK, booted up the word processing program, and stared at the blank computer screen for a while. Some authors complain about writer's block, but I'll let you in on a little secret: there are times when the blankness of the page (in my case a video tube) is a great comfort. You stare at the emptiness and become part of it, a clean slate, a fresh start. Anything can still happen. The idea, of course, is that after you've emptied yourself the creative reservoir can again fill with fresh images, new stories. Sometimes it doesn't work that way, and you have to get away from the blank page and go out into the world.

I call it having the itch.

For me the only way to scratch it is to get the van out of the garage and see how much havoc I can wreak in the madness of Boston traffic. With that in mind I got on Huntington Avenue and rode it southwest to the tow yard where the remains of Sully's car had been impounded for forensic investigation by the Bomb Squad.

The customized van is equipped with a lift that lowers me to ground level without any fuss. My wheelchair is fitted with a pair of knobby tires that get me over most curbs, potholes, and door treads. In other words, I get around, relying on upper body strength and a certain amount of cunning. As I've mentioned, Meg, with two perfectly perfect legs, often has to jog to keep up with me. If that sounds like bragging, so be it.

The tall, stooped black gentleman who met me at the chain-link gate of the tow yard was one Alvin Zamboni, known to friends and enemies alike, he said, as Bones.

"You have a lot of enemies, Bones?"

"Hey, man," he said, chuckling, "I work at the city tow yard, you dig? Most days the only person don't hate me is my wife, and I'm never really positive she don't, neither."

Bones was willing to let me look at the remains of Sully's car so long as I didn't get close enough to tamper with any evidence.

"They tell me the dude was in that car is gonna be okay. If that a fact, he one lucky son of a gun. I'm sayin' it a miracle he survive, you dig? That car be blowed to *smithereens,* man. Ain't hardly nothin' left."

Bones wasn't exaggerating. All that remained of the vehicle was the charred chassis and a portion of the rear seat and trunk. The whole front end was in pieces, which the forensic investigators had laid out and numbered with grease pencil. The steering column and wheel were charred and partially melted, and what remained of the front seat was scorched.

"The miracle," I said to Bones, "is that he wasn't in the car when it blew. Couldn't have been. He must have been walking away when it went off," I added, remembering the fragments of glass that had been dug out of his backside, and his semiconscious raving about being airborne.

"Makes sense," Bones said, nodding. "Otherwise the dude be in as many pieces as the car. You smell it, man?"

I sniffed. There was an odor of charred paint, and another, sharper smell I couldn't identify.

"Jelly," Bones said. "That a gelignite bomb. Potassium nitrate."

"You can tell by the odor?"

"Ain't nothin' else stink like it do, man. Smell hot even now, when it all cooled down. All it take, two, three pounds of jelly. Mix it up right in the kitchen, if you know how, just like Momma make a cake." He paused and sighed, adding, "It a dangerous world we live in, man, you ever think about that?"

"I do, Bones," I said. "I do indeed."

The young lady at the reception desk at Beth Israel was very cooperative. Too cooperative, in my opinion.

"Mr. Sullivan is in room 684," she said, consulting her records. "When you exit the elevator on the sixth floor, turn left and look for corridor B."

"That's it?" I said. "You don't want my name? Any identification?"

She smiled pleasantly. "Not necessary."

"What I meant is, isn't there some kind of security in place for Lieutenant Sullivan?"

"Pardon?"

"You mean to tell me the patient isn't under guard?"

The young lady shook her head and looked puzzled. "Should he be?"

"Never mind," I said, and wheeled to the elevator.

The car was slow to respond, which gave me a chance to rehearse. I was going to read the riot act to Larry Sheehan. Nothing but craven incompetence could explain leaving Tim Sullivan unguarded—someone had already tried to kill him once, and another attempt wasn't exactly inconceivable. And as I had unwittingly demonstrated, any damn fool, or killer, for that matter, could saunter up to the reception desk and cheerfully be given directions to Sully's room.

Eventually the elevator doors opened. I spun around and wheeled in backwards. I was about to punch in the floor number when a flower shop deliveryman slipped into the car, clutching a tall vase of yellow mums. The deliveryman, wearing heavily tinted glasses, a cap, and a sky blue jumpsuit, gave me a brittle smile and turned his back. The legend between his shoulder blades read *Flower Power, Inc.,* which neatly sums up what happened to the worst minds of my generation.

I hesitated when the elevator opened on the sixth floor, trying to remember which way to turn for corridor B. Mr. Flower Power went around me to the left, holding the big vase of mums out like a trophy, and I found myself following his Reeboks.

I trailed him right to the door marked 684. He was well ahead of me and already approaching the bed when I wheeled through the door into the private room. Curtains had been drawn around the bed. Familiar as I was with hospital routine, I assumed Sully was getting his bandages changed, or maybe his bedpan. The flower deliveryman wasn't deterred, however. Neither snow nor rain nor the prospect of a frosty nurse was going to delay the precious gift of chrysanthemums to the designated patient.

Holding the vase in the crook of one arm, the deliveryman quickly swept open the curtain with his right hand. He partially obscured my view, but I could see that Sully wasn't there in the bed.

Larry Sheehan was. Sitting on top of the covers fully dressed and cradling his service revolver in his lap.

"Hey, ain't that sweet?" he said, grinning. "Pretty flowers." His voice hardened. "Now put 'em down on the table there and show me some ID."

The deliveryman hesitated. I almost had time to feel sorry for him, running up against a hard case like Sheehan. Then he lost my sympathy by reaching into the vase and pulling out a .44 caliber handgun, equipped with a long black silencer.

Things began to happen very fast. Sheehan rolled off the bed and dropped to the floor. Flower Power squeezed off a couple of rounds. The silenced gun made a coughing sound and parts of the mattress exploded.

Then Flower Power turned to leave and saw me. I was suddenly very conscious of the fact that I was blocking the door. He hesitated for a heartbeat: Should he fire, or would it be quicker to grab the chair and yank me out of the way?

"Drop the weapon!" Larry Sheehan was on his feet, disheveled but unharmed, extending the .38 with both hands. "Drop it!"

Flower Power had a different idea. He spun around, firing as he turned. A window blew out. Sheehan squeezed off two shots. One of them hit the wall, penetrated, and was eventually found embedded in the base of a water cooler. The other slug hit Flower Power in the clavicle, then passed through the left chamber of his heart, rupturing the aorta, and finally lodged in his lungs. I learned that later, from the autopsy report.

Also noted at the inquest was the fact that the victim had several freshly broken ribs. That happened moments after he died, when Larry Sheehan screamed, "You stupid fuck!" and kicked him. The tinted glasses came loose and skittered away, revealing a pair of newly vacant brown eyes.

"I tole him to drop it, right?" Sheehan said, turning to me.

I nodded by way of agreement.

"Guy musta been crazy," he said, falling to his knees beside the corpse and going through the drill of looking for identification. "Jeez," he said, indicating the weapon clutched in the dead man's hand, "a silencer. I never seen one except on TV."

The use of my voice returned. I said, "He must have been a professional hit man."

"Nah," Sheehan said, as plainclothes cops began to converge on the room. "If he was a pro I'da been wacked. You, too, prob'ly. What we got here is some kind of nut case."

As it happened, both of us were right. The would-be assassin was a professional killer with a history of mental disturbance, although a fair amount of dogged investigation was required before his identity was confirmed.

After preliminary questioning by the Internal Affairs Unit, whose duty it was to check out any weapons discharged by a police officer, I was granted permission to visit Tim Sullivan. He was registered under an assumed name in the psychiatric wing of the hospital, where dangerous or deranged patients are temporarily confined pending transfer to more secure facilities. Sully wasn't happy with his situation there, although he had to agree the precautions Sheehan had insisted on were, as it turned out, very prudent indeed.

"I have the world's biggest headache," he complained, indicating the lumps on the back of his head, and the dressing over his stitches. "All night long there's some loony raving in the next room. They had to put restraints on him, finally."

"Yeah, I said. "It's tough getting sleep in a hospital. Not that you should be squawking. I saw the remains of your car, Sully. By rights, you ought to be in a nice quiet drawer in the morgue."

Sully gave me a sour look. He was in a chair beside the bed, sitting on the soft plastic ring that was supposed to make it easier on his wounded backside. With the horn-rimmed glasses and the thinning hair and the slight build he looked more like a distraught schoolteacher than a decorated homicide detective. Owing to the doctors' concern about a possible concussion he was wired to the life monitoring system, and the encumbrance clearly irritated him.

"I suppose you want to hear the whole story," he said in an accusing tone.

"If it's not too much trouble."

"This is the whole story: I went out to start the car. I did so. I got out to lower the garage door. Then I remembered I hadn't set out the garbage pail. I was walking over to pick it up when all of a sudden I was flying through the air. Next thing, as the saying goes, everything went blank."

"That's all you remember?"

"The sum and total," he said, fidgeting on the plastic ring. "Now it's your turn. Describe the guy Sheehan popped."

"Early thirties. Five ten, medium build. Maybe a little extra bulk in the chest and shoulders, like he'd worked with weights. Short brown hair. Clean shaven. Brown eyes. Fair complexion, with some pockmarks. Size ten shoes. Right handed. No visible scars or tattoos, although his sleeves were long, so I can't be sure of that."

Sully nodded. "Could be any one of a million guys.

You're the clever crime writer. Can't you come up with a distinguishing characteristic?"

"Sure," I said. "He's been shot dead. That ought to narrow it down some."

He smiled, then grimaced in pain. "My butt was peppered with broken glass," he said. "I'd prefer to stand, but that makes me dizzy."

"Could have been a lot worse," I said.

He looked at me and my wheelchair. "Yeah," he said. "I guess it could at that."

I decided to change the subject. "Sheehan continues to amaze me," I said. "I thought he was screwing up, but it turns out he was right on top of the thing."

Sully nodded thoughtfully. "You saw it go down. Was he justified in discharging his weapon?"

"Absolutely."

"No doubt in your mind?"

I shrugged. "I've got all kinds of doubts in my mind, but none of them are about Larry Sheehan returning fire. It was shoot or be shot."

"Remember that," Sully said, "the next time your pals in the media characterize the detective as 'Shoot First Sheehan.'"

"That was Mike Barnicle for the *Globe*," I said, "and if you'd bothered to read beyond the headline, he said he was writing to praise Larry, not to bury him, or words to that effect."

Sully appeared satisfied. He also looked exhausted. I said good-bye and was pushing out the door when he called me back.

"You get any telephone calls about that movie they're making? I mean anonymous calls? Female voice?"

"No," I said. "Did you?"

"Later."

He was asleep when I left.

*   *   *

She knelt before the dark altar, alone except for her angels, her Voices. It was a time of mourning. Mourning the death of one who had served the left hand of God. The mercenary. He who had been the executioner of her will, and who had died in the line of duty.

Another man killed by a conspiracy of cops. No matter. A slight delay. She had other servants, other powers. She lit a taper, touched it to one candle, then another, until all of them were lit. The wicks sputtered and smoked, but the tiny flames failed to illuminate the enormous darkness.

She prayed: "Revenge is mine, sayeth the Lord."

CHAPTER FOUR

WE WERE HAVING DINNER OUT ON THE DECK when trouble called. I was tending to the marinated chicken breasts sizzling on the charcoal grill and at the same time gloating about not being stuck in the traffic on Storrow Drive, which brushes the north side of our building. Beyond the stream of vehicles the Charles River was mirror calm, a reflecting basin for the Cambridge skyline. Megan was sprawled in the lounge, a summer tan glowing on her long, slender limbs, her thick mop of hair fanning out like an auburn halo.

"Ken and Barb Commuter will be an hour just getting onto the expressway," I said, turning the chicken. "All that trouble to live in the 'burbs. And what do they get? They get to paint the house. They get to mow the lawn. They get to cook designer pork chops on self-tending mesquite grills."

Meg gave me one of her looks. "So in your opinion carbon monoxide is superior to mesquite smoke?"

"No question," I said.

It was about then that the lobby buzzer sounded. Meg went inside to answer and leaned back through the door to say, "Russ White would like a word. Okay by you?"

"Sure," I said, "why not?"

While Meg went to unlock the hallway door, I wheeled into the kitchen to mix drinks. Russ White writes crime features for the *Boston Standard* the chain-owned tabloid that plays bratty kid brother to the bigger, better, and slightly stuck-up *Globe*. Russ and I had been exchanging favors for a number of years, and I wasn't sure where we stood at the moment. Quite possibly I was in his debt; whatever the balance, he undoubtedly wanted more than a few words and a cool drink.

I made three tall vodka and sodas, with a twist of lime. I was in a tangy, twisted mood. Partly it was the prospect of dealing with a blood and guts reporter like Russ White. Partly it was the aftershock of having been within touching distance of sudden death earlier in the day.

The smell of cordite can be a wicked thing, as seductive as opium. If you're a sedentary type like myself, attuned to nuances of word and gesture, the sudden influx of adrenaline does more than stimulate the nerves. It charges the inner batteries. It invigorates the psyche. The thrill itself has resonance. And if, like me, you already have a bullet in your spine, the craving for violence and danger is doubly disturbing.

Mary Kean, who edits my Casey novels, has a theory that all crime writers are criminals at heart, that we sublimate antisocial tendencies by creating page after blood-spattered page. I find that I cannot entirely disagree with the theory, and that, too, disturbs me.

I made the vodkas taller still, slipped them into a carrier, and returned to the deck. Russ White is a slender man who tries to dress dapper and always manages to look slightly rumpled despite the quality of his clothing.

He has a thin face, large, active brown eyes, a pockmarked complexion, and a jutting bottom lip. His rusty hair is starting to show streaks of silver. When I wheeled onto the deck he was standing with his hands deep in the pockets of his beige linen trousers, watching Meg smother a small grease fire on the grill. She grimaced at the reporter and said, "I hope you like blackened chicken."

"Hey," he said, "black is beautiful. Isn't that right, Jack?"

"Russ, since when did you wear suspenders and a bow tie?"

He grinned, snapping the black suspenders. "Since Devlin started wearing them."

Devlin was the *Standard*'s flashy young publisher. A business school wunderkind who fraternized with the Boston social elite, attending fund raisers and charity functions. Canny and ruthless. Russ liked to say that he and Devlin had a loathe-hate relationship, which the reporter clearly relished.

"Last year it was the Reeboks," he said, taking a drink from the tray. "Remember when all the boomer execs were wearing overpriced sneakers along with their nine-hundred-dollar London power suits? Devlin gets himself a pair of 'Boks, right away I get a pair at discount. Drives him nuts, right? Only he doesn't want to let on it bothers him. After a suitable interval he puts away the running shoes and starts wearing these lizard-skin loafers. He knows I can't keep up, since he had to fly to Rome to buy them. Guy'll do anything to maintain the edge." Russ flicked the red bow tie and winked. "Tomorrow he'll be back to the silk rep and one of those pricey snakeskin belts. The little battles, Jack, that's what I live for."

Russ leisurely finished one vodka and then another,

nibbling potato salad and scorched chicken from a paper plate. I was almost convinced his visit was purely social after all, when he licked his fingers and casually mentioned that the identity of the man who had tried to kill Tim Sullivan was still unknown, some six hours after the incident.

"No wallet, clothing labels removed, serial numbers on the weapon filed off," he said. "They have his fingerprints, of course, and a cast of his dental work. A name will turn up eventually. Why I mention it, I thought maybe you could identify the deceased. You know how Devlin gets about a hot cop story. He wants a name."

I said, "How about John Doe?"

"Hey," Russ said, affecting an apologetic tone. "You were there. You saw the perpetrator."

"Who told you I was there?"

Russ made a zipping motion over his lips.

"Had to be Sheehan," I said, "or Gallo, come to think of it."

"Gee," Russ said, "since when are you so bashful? 'Boston Author on Scene as Cop Assassin Is Gunned Down.' Has a nice ring to it. Might help sell a few more books. Maybe jack up the ratings for the TV movie, come to think of it."

Coming from anybody else, I'd have been insulted. But Russ was just doing his job, trying to get me to rise to the bait. He was looking for a slant, a quote, a lead— anything to help give his story that loud tabloid sizzle.

"Russ," I said. "I'm going to use a word that is not in your vocabulary. The word is *coincidence*. It is defined as 'the occurrence of events at the same time by accident.' I went to the hospital to visit Tim Sullivan, a friend who happens to be a homicide detective. I had no idea Larry Sheehan was setting a trap for the hired gun, whoever he was. I happened to be in the building when it went down. Coincidence, pure and simple."

Russ nodded. "So you won't tell me the killer's name?"

I looked at Megan. She shook her head in disbelief, amused and a little stunned at the bluntness of the reporter's interrogation.

"Okay," I sighed. "His name is Lee Harvey Oswald. It was all part of a vast global conspiracy."

Russ finished his second tall vodka and soda and requested something with caffeine. Meg brought out a pitcher of iced coffee and, smiling still, offered to pour it over his head if he didn't stop abusing our hospitality.

"Jack has nothing to do with this one," she said. "He has nothing to hide. So get it through that thick skull of yours."

The reporter, who knew Megan well enough to realize she was fully capable of making good on her threat, smile or no smile, prudently drew his canvas chair out of range.

"My big mouth," he said, flipping open his notepad. "How do you spell *coincidence*?"

Megan poured him a glass of the iced coffee. He added sugar and absentmindedly stirred it with a yellow pencil. "It's just there are these rumors," he said, looking from Meg to the pitcher, ready to duck. "Your name came up, Jack. I had to check it out."

"What kind of rumors?"

"Interesting ones," he said. "The Weasel is letting it slip that Sully had an affair with a mobster's wife."

"Delaney said that?"

"Words to that effect."

Liam Delaney, the commissioner's white-haired, back-slapping deputy, was notorious for dealing in half-truths. No doubt that was why he'd been put in charge of public relations. Knowing Tim Sullivan's rigid code about not fraternizing with known criminals or their associates, I didn't really believe even half of the rumor. But if Sully *had* put horns on a Mafia boss, that would explain the bomb in the car and the Flower Power gunman sneaking into the hospital room to finish the job.

"The Weasel say what mobster, in particular?"

"He implied one of the Calvino brothers."

"Christ almighty."

"Yeah," Russ said. "Sully'll need more than Jesus on his side if he's getting it on with a Calvino woman. Wife, daughter, or mistress, it wouldn't make much difference."

The Calvino family owned the mob franchise in the North End. All three brothers were out on bail, pending various grand jury indictments, and had been for as long as I could remember. Mob killings were usually covered by the Organized Crime Unit, but since Sully was the chief homicide investigator, it was not unusual for him to be consulted, especially if a particular case was what cops call a mystery—a murder by assailants unknown. That possibility had given rise to another, more credible rumor, Russ asserted.

"This I heard from a lady works for a well-known criminal lawyer," he said, leaning back in his chair. "A criminal lawyer in the sense that he is on retainer to certain gentlemen of the Mafia persuasion, and in the sense that he personally dabbles in high-ticket loansharking. Anyhow, this lady has a nice set, you know?"

"A nice set of what?" Megan asked, grinning.

"Ears," Russ said, clearing his throat and blushing faintly. "Very acute hearing. She overheard a conversation, the substance of which was, there is a cop lieutenant who has some very damaging evidence that might actually cause the special prosecutor to empanel a jury and bring one of the brothers to trial."

"At long last."

"No names were mentioned," Russ said. "But if the lieutenant is Sullivan, and if he has convincing testimony, they might try to pop him. Killing a cop would be a dumb move, but no one ever accused the Calvino brothers of belonging to Mensa."

"Those are big ifs," I said. "You sure you weren't distracted by the lady's attractive pair of ears?"

"Hey, I said it was a rumor, okay? I thought maybe you could confirm or deny."

"It's up to Sully to confirm or deny, Russ. You know that."

"So," the reporter said, "The lieutenant never mentioned a mob case he was working? Or a mob lady? Never said he'd been threatened, or was in fear of his life?"

"Not to me."

"Never mentioned a series of anonymous phone calls, somehow connected to your movie?"

A skilled reporter will do that, rattle off a number of "normal" questions, then drop the bombshell, hoping to catch you off balance. I almost fell for it.

"No comment," I finally said. "Except it's not 'my' movie, Russ. I merely wrote the book it is vaguely—very vaguely—based on."

"Yeah?" he said, lifting his pencil from the notebook and meeting my eyes. "I thought you wrote the screenplay."

"An early draft. Since cut up and rewritten by the director."

"And you don't know anything about a woman who's been calling up Sullivan and complaining about real events depicted in the movie?"

"Correct," I said. "I don't know anything. Furthermore it sounds preposterous. The original script wasn't based on any real events, or real crimes. And from what

I've seen, the shooting script isn't based on any real characters, either. Far from it."

"So *Casey and the Black Widow* isn't about a mob figure, or a mob-related crime?"

"It's *Casey and the Black Widow* now," I said ruefully, "and the only mob figure in it is Smilin' Stan Seigel, a bookie. I made him up. He doesn't exist in any real shape or form, by that name or any other. No one in the book or the movie resembles any of the Calvino brothers, to answer your next question. The studio lawyers made sure of that before they okayed the production."

Russ White sighed and flipped the notebook closed. The unwary will sometimes assume that means the interview is over, and what follows is off the record. Aware of his technique, I was ready for the next question.

"It's just the name of Lenny Calvino keeps coming up," Russ said wearily, "and if you didn't know what a dull skunk Fat Lenny really is, you might assume he's one of those colorful gangster types you all the time see in the movies. He's got, what, two ex-wives? He's got a current missus, also a couple chippies he keeps around for whenever he has the urge. So if your pal Sullivan got himself involved with a Calvino-connected woman, it could have been someone in Fat Lenny's harem. The other two brothers, Frank and Tony, they keep much lower profiles."

Megan laughed. "A Sicilian harem," she said. "I think that's a mixed metaphor."

"Must be tough," Russ observed, "living with an editor."

I followed the reporter to the door, unwilling to let him have the last word.

"I think you're barking up the wrong tree, Russ," I said. "Larry Sheehan doesn't think it was a professional hit. He thinks the guy was a nut case."

He shrugged, jamming at the button for the elevator. "Sheehan has his opinions," he said. "I have mine."

At half past eleven Megan was in bed, reading a manuscript. As I've observed to her, anyone clutching a blue pencil is not quite naked, no matter how bare the flesh. I was in the study, ostensibly making notes for the Casey novel I was supposed to be working on. What I was really doing was doodling on a yellow pad and listening to Eric Jackson's nightly jazz show. The acoustic spotlight was on Bill Evans, and it was easy to lose myself in the cool, lucid notes rising from Evans's keyboard. The purity of the music made my thoughts clear, helped me get the priorities in order, and I was about to go in and strip away Meg's blue pencil when the phone rang.

It was Lindy Bangs.

"We missed you today, Jack," she said. "I thought you wanted to watch us shoot the fire escape scene?"

I decided to give her the short version of what had happened at the hospital.

"I was visiting a sick friend."

"Pretty lame," Lindy said. There was something in the sultry tone of her voice that made me think she was high on something. Dope or booze, maybe a little of each. "You can do better than that. Invent some sort of thrilling adventure, like in your books."

"Nah," I said. "Nothing exciting ever happens to me. Seriously, Lindy, the movie is your baby. I've gotten used to the idea, finally. Having the author hanging around the set is a pain in the ass, right?"

"Not you," she said. "You've been sweet. Why I'm calling is, we're having some trouble with the continuity. You might be able to help."

"Yeah?" I said, doubtfully. "I was under the impression the shooting script was graven in stone. 'Thou shalt not alter a line,' I think that's what you told me."

"Talking through my hat," she said. "In point of fact, we have a consultation clause in your contract. I'm going to invoke it. All I want you to do is come by the shoot tomorrow at noon, check over a couple pages of dialogue, maybe give me a few ideas how we can clean it up."

"Why the change of heart, Lindy?"

"No change, honey," she said. "I just want to take advantage of you while I've got the chance."

Megan was sitting up in bed, wearing an expectant expression and nothing else.

"Lindy Bangs," I said, unbuttoning my shirt. "Wants to know if I'm available."

"Funny," Meg said, smiling with a tinge of wickedness. "I've been wondering the same thing myself."

The streetlights made the shadows strange. Shapes that might, in a heartbeat, reach up from the pavement and drag her down into the darkness. This was Beacon Street, and once she had walked here with her lover, holding hands in the sunlight. She cherished the pain of that memory, as one would a wound received in valiant battle.

She watched the building on the corner until the lights on the top floor went out. The man in the wheelchair lived there.

The teller of tales. The liar.

Were the Voices directing her to him? Was he, like his friend the lieutenant detective, to be chosen?

She remembered that the man in the wheelchair carried a sacrament, a glowing host: a small, sacred piece of lead in his spine. The cop bullet that put him in the chair was a reminder.

She prayed he would not forget.

CHAPTER FIVE

SULLY ROSE AGAIN ON THE THIRD DAY. THIS was against the advice of the attending physicians, who made him sign a disclaimer before releasing him. I found him in the tiny garden behind his home in the Jamaica Plain section of the city. He was lying on a webbed lounger, a sun hat covering his face. The bandages around his chest and abdomen made him look oddly bulky.

"You need a lube job," he said without removing the hat from his face. "Your wheels are squeaking."

"Thanks, I'm fine," I said. "And how are you?"

While parking the van, I'd noticed two unmarked detective sedans, one on the corner and the other curbside with the motor running. A police cruiser was taking up the slot in Sully's driveway, where the black scars of the explosion were still visible on the concrete slab. The windows in the garage door were boarded over with new plywood. A patrolman stood in the trellised doorway, armed with a walkie-talkie and a shotgun. The message to any would-be assassin was clear: go away, the place is covered.

"I've got a headache," Sully said.

"Probably the result of talking through your hat."

He removed the hat and squinted at me. I noticed another uniformed cop in the backyard, partially obscured by an intervening rhododendron bush. Since his mother's death, Sully had let the place grow wild, except for a small patch of grass that he kept reasonably short with a push mower.

"You think they'll try again?" I asked, eyeing the guard.

Sully plopped the hat back over his face, affecting disgust. "Who's 'they'? There was only the one, and Sheehan shot him, bless his heart."

A woman with frosted hair came out of the house, carrying a lawn umbrella. The nurse. She was not in uniform, but had an unmistakable air of nurturing, and the unfortunate habit of speaking in the first-person plural.

"We must remember about the antibiotics," she said, planting the pointed end of the umbrella into the grass and setting it up. "One of the side effects is increased sensitivity to ultraviolet light. We must avoid direct sunlight," she added, and then marched back into the house.

"You hear that, Jack?" Sully said, sitting up. "I'm like a damn houseplant."

"*Timothious Sullivania*," I said. "Prefers the shade. Very hearty variety, capable of withstanding violent explosions."

"Not to mention bad jokes," he muttered.

"Sorry," I said. "You still feel pretty rotten, huh?"

"Bruised and battered," he said. "Poked and prodded. You know what it's like."

I did indeed. Six interminably long months in the paraplegic ward of Mass General Hospital ran like a livid scar through my memory. In contrast, Sully hadn't done so bad. He'd walked away from it. The difference, of course, was that his was no accident. Two attempts had been made upon his life, and I wanted to know why he was so convinced there would not be a third.

"Told you," he said. "Sheehan nailed him."

I said, "What about the woman?"

Sully leveled his pale blue eyes at me. I felt like a kid who'd been caught cheating on a catechism test, and was about to feel the steel edge of a nun's ruler.

"What woman?" he said.

"The woman who threatened you over the phone. Don't shake your head, Sul. You know exactly what I'm talking about. When I saw you in the hospital you asked me if I'd gotten any anonymous calls from a woman regarding the Casey movie. Implying you *had* gotten such calls."

He looked sly. "Must have been off my nut. All the drugs they pumped into me."

"Something's going on, and if it's got anything to do with the Casey movie, or with me, I want to know about it."

Sullivan sighed and carefully readjusted himself on the lounge, moving like an old man. He picked up a small bell and gave it a shake. The nurse responded immediately, as if she'd been waiting just inside the screen door.

"Iced tea and two aspirin for me," he said. "Mr. Hawkins would probably like a beer right about now, but since we're fresh out, he'll settle for iced tea. Okay?"

"Tea is fine," I said.

"And ask the officer what he wants," Sully directed. "The one over there, skulking in the rhododendrons."

The deliberate manner meant Sully had decided to confide in me, as much as he ever confided in anyone. He always kept something back; that was his way. He waited until the refreshments had been delivered and the nurse had again retreated into the house.

"Two weeks ago I get the first call. My immediate reaction is the lady on the other end of the line has made the wrong connection. She says, 'My love can't sleep, his eyes are open.' I said what you'd expect—sorry, you must have the wrong number. Was just about to hang up when she addresses me by name." Sully looked at the two aspirin the nurse had dropped into his hand, but made no move to take them. "'Lieutenant Detective Tim Sullivan, Homicide Unit,' she says. Like she wants it very clear she hasn't made an error, called one of the twenty other Tim Sullivans in the book. Like a fool I respond, 'How may I help you?' That makes her laugh. And this is a lady with a peculiar kind of laugh, Jack. Not a funny laugh at all. The shivering kind of laugh, you know what I mean?"

"I think I do," I said.

"Next thing she says is, 'My television is broken, I can't turn off the voices.'"

"Uh-oh," I said.

"Right," Sully said, flicking the aspirin to the ground. "Sounds like a schizo. I'm about to hang up the phone, but something about her tone made me want to hear what she had to say, crazy as it was. Not that she made a lot of sense. Her sentences were all chopped up. Words in the wrong place. Kept going on about the voices and the itchy things in her head. Finally I told her to call the community health hotline. I even gave her the number."

"How did she react?"

"The laugh again. *Very* creepy, okay? Then she says,

'You're going to be in the movie, I saw it on TV.' Then she hung up."

"Saw it on TV?"

"The news, Jack. That was the night they had a little segment on how they were about to start filming your Casey movie in Back Bay."

I started to say how it wasn't my movie, and stopped. It wasn't a distinction that Sully would appreciate, especially since he was well aware of the commonly held opinion that he was the model for the fictional Lieutenant Casey.

"I don't recall that your name was mentioned on that segment," I said. "Hell, it ran less than thirty seconds."

"Television is a powerful medium," he said sarcastically. "Especially if the voices persist after you pull the plug."

"She's off her rocker, whoever she is. She call again?"

He nodded. "Five times so far. Once at three in the morning. That was a cute one. She says, 'Lieutenant Timothy Sullivan, you have a sacred heart. I'm going to paint it black.'"

"Paint it black?"

"Spooky, huh? She started chanting, over and over. 'Paint it black, paint it black.' Sounded like a prayer, almost."

When I asked if he'd put a trace on the calls he made a face. "Come on, Jack. You know better. Go to court and get a warrant because some loony wants to tell me about the voices in her TV set? Never happen. Judge would advise me to get an unlisted number."

"So why didn't you?" I asked.

He shrugged. "There's something about the lady. I can't explain it. I guess maybe I thought I could help her somehow. Not any more, though. Not since the bomb."

"You think there's a connection?"

Sully sat up and leaned forward, grimacing in pain. "You tell me," he said, keeping his voice low. "The last time she called, it was right before I went out to start the car. And you know what she says?"

I shook my head.

"She says, 'I just wanted to say good-bye.' I was still thinking about that weird laugh when the car blew up."

The members of the film crew were eating lunch under a tent on the riverside Embankment area. The food was supplied by All Things Bountiful, a trendy Newbury Street caterer that specialized in shredded, salady stuff. Lots of nuts and sprouts were in evidence. There was, in my opinion, an unfortunate lack of cheeseburgers.

When I arrived Lindy Bangs was seated a little away from the main congregation with Clarence Higgs, the production whiz, and Burt Bardo, the actor who was portraying Casey. Lindy was stirring a cup of yogurt and going over street diagrams with Higgs while her assistant director, a willowy young man of about twenty, made notes.

"They want a three-car smash," she was saying. "We'll give them a three-car smash. Do you have any problem with that?"

Higgs, a sour-faced, graying man of forty or so, jabbed his finger at the diagram on the table. "What I'm saying, dear, is fine, we can do a three-car, we can do a *six*-car, only it has to be budgeted."

"Oh," Lindy said, running creamy white fingers through her mop of fuchsine red hair. "I was under the impression it *was* fully budgeted, Clarence, darling. I believe you signed off on it, matter of fact."

"Right. Correct. I signed based on the line item, which specified a lower per diem for the police detail. I get here, the cop union is on our ass first thing. Result is that the accountants agreed to a higher per diem rate, okay? So the cost of a three-car smash goes up an extra twenty-five hundred."

"Clarence," Lindy sighed, "what's the prob?"

"The *problem*," Clarence said, "is I can't authorize the stunt until you sign the new voucher."

"Why didn't you say so?"

He rolled his eyes. She signed the voucher. Burt Bardo winked at me and then nudged Lindy. "Author on the set," he said, adopting a mock-warning tone. "Secure the shooting scripts, uncue the cue cards."

"Oh, *hello,*" Lindy said. "This is a nice surprise."

"You asked me to come by at noon," I said uneasily. "For a conference. Something about fixing a few pages of dialogue."

"I did?"

"Honest," I said. "Cross my heart."

"Oh, I mean of *course* I did. Only we fixed it already. Sorry, Willis should have called you."

Her assistant looked up from his notebook and made a point of not meeting my eyes. "Left a message on his machine," he said. "Lindy, we need to go over the sequence checklists. Harvey is having a bird."

"Excuse me, Jack."

Lindy blew me a kiss and went off with her arm draped around Willis.

Burt Bardo watched her walking away and said, "Let me guess. You got the urgent call after ten o'clock."

"Midnight," I said.

"The thing is, after ten Lindy enters the Twilight Zone. She gets telephonitis."

Unlike Casey, or Tim Sullivan, for that matter, Burt Bardo was several inches over six feet tall and strikingly handsome. With his thick, swept-back hair and deeply clefted chin, he looked more like a prime-time doctor than a homicide cop. In his mid-fifties, he was also about two decades older than I pictured Casey. I didn't, however, begrudge him his looks or his age. Of the several actors I'd met since shooting started, Burt was the least "actorish." Maybe because he had been a minor star for a goodly number of years, and had no need to exert himself off camera. I was mildly surprised to discover he'd actually read several of the Casey books, unlike Lindy Bangs, who worked up her script from a studio synopsis.

Bardo lit up one of the small Dutch cigars that he inhaled like cigarettes, and said, "First day of shooting I get a late-night buzz from the dear girl, who has decided absolutely that I must play Casey with a mustache. This will necessitate reshooting the first few pages. I say fine, if that's what you want, and the next morning I tell make up to apply the 'stash. I step out of the trailer and she gives me this blank look, like what am I doing with that hairy thing on my upper lip? Lindy's forgotten all about the call, we're not reshooting, how could I possibly think she would go over budget simply to establish a mustache?"

"It's no big deal," I said. "Just a phone call. Is Willis her boyfriend?"

Bardo laughed. "Willis is Clarence's boyfriend. Or he was. I heard they had a tiff. Far as I know Lindy Bangs is currently solo."

"I can't figure her out."

"Take an old ham's advice," he said, patting my hand. "Don't try."

CHAPTER SIX

FOUR DAYS LATER I LEARNED THE LATE Flower Power's name was Leland Maddock and he lived, or had, in a two-room basement flat in Dorchester. Sergeant Detective Larry Sheehan made the first identification, later corroborated through a print match by the U.S. Marine Corps, which had given Maddock a psychiatric discharge, and the Veterans Hospital, where he had been an outpatient.

Sheehan asked me to meet him at McCann's Bar & Grill, a Washington Street cop hangout. I found him settled onto a stool at the counter, working on a beer and smoking a Lucky Strike.

"There was six vehicles abandoned in the hospital parking facility," he said, explaining how he'd made the ID. "Two was on the VRS sheet—that's Vehicles Reported Stolen, in case you forgot—so I decided to check out the other four first. Make a long story short, it turns out the Chevy Nova, which has an alarm system, is registered to one Leland Maddock, of St. Jude Street. Nothing in the phone book, so I check out his address. The landlady, a Mrs. McGillicuddy—I swear on the Bible, that's really her name—she ain't seen him in a week. Tells me he's very quiet and considerate. Mrs. McGillicuddy thinks he's quiet because she's deaf as a haddock. The considerate is because he took her trash out to the curb every Thursday. What a sweet kid, huh?"

Sheehan peeled the label from his beer bottle and pasted it to the linoleum countertop. It was early in the afternoon and McCann's was deserted except for Sheehan, myself, and the bartender, who was studying the racing form with the intensity of a law student preparing for the bar. A cool September rain streaked the grimy bar windows and washed some of the filth from the Washington Street gutters.

"I show her the morgue shot of the suspect," Sheehan was saying. "She makes him right away. 'That's Leland, but why's he smiling like that? I never seen him smile like that.' So I tell her he wasn't feeling no pain when the picture got took, and that's a fact."

"She let you into his place?"

"Sure she did. I turned on the Sheehan charm."

"You didn't need a warrant?"

"Give me a break," he said. "The guy is dead. We ain't planning to arrest him."

After finishing the beer Sheehan had coffee from a steel pot that had been simmering for most of a decade. I passed on the gray-looking stuff, and declined Larry's kind offer to buy me a pickled egg.

"You ever see *Alien*? Had eyes just like that," I pointed out as he nibbled the gelatinous egg.

"Yeah," Sheehan said, grinning as he took a bigger bite. "You're one of them what only eats stuff they invented in France. Croissants and shit."

"Croissants and *merde*."

"Don't think I don't get it, Professor, 'cause I do."

We were waiting for Tim Sullivan. The game plan was that both Sully and I would follow Sheehan to St. Jude Street. Sullivan, naturally, wanted to make an inspection of the perpetrator's residence. He had requested that I come along because newspaper clippings had been found, referring to the made-for-TV Casey movie. Implying that I might be able to shed some light on why the suspect had had such clippings in his possession. I hadn't liked the implication, but had agreed to go along to satisfy my own curiosity.

"Wait'll you see the place," Sheehan said. "This guy Maddock was one wacked-out ex-jarhead, let me tell ya. Sure had a lot of reading material, though. Regular bookworm," he added, and then refused to explain what he meant, assuring me that I would find out, "in good due time, if the lieutenant approves."

The rain had increased to a downpour by the time Sully arrived and tooted his horn from the curb. In the minute or so it took me to get into the van, using the power lift, I got soaked to the skin. Sheehan looked similarly drenched when our three vehicles converged on the Dorchester residence of the late Leland Maddock.

"Freakin' rain," he said, using a key the landlady had provided to let us into the vestibule.

Sully, who with his broken and heavily taped ribs was in no shape to assist, stood by while Sheehan helped me negotiate the twelve steps down to the basement apartment.

"I'm warning you," Sheehan said. "Breathe easy in here. The place stinks."

When he had unlocked and opened the inner door, I got the first acrid whiff of Leland Maddock's private world: the strong, intermingled odors of burned candle wax, rotting vegetables, and urine. Sheehan flipped on the lights. The immediate visual impression was of a squalid mess. Soiled clothing and garbage were strewn through two small rooms. The place was overflowing with cardboard boxes, trash, empty beer cans. Candy wrappers were scattered like dead leaves over a forest green carpet. And the candles. The candles were everywhere. Perched on the stacks of magazines, on the arms of a tattered easy chair, on the mottled rug, on tables, on the counter in the kitchenette area.

Maddock's decorating effort was limited to a big poster on the wall above the TV set. A large, menacing Rambo, armed with enough ordinance to outfit a SWAT team, glared from a jungle setting. Maddock's reading material, as evidenced by the scattered piles of books and magazines, was confined to military and weapons magazines and various publications like *The U.S. Navy Seal Combat Manual, The Anarchist Cookbook,* and an intriguing little pamphlet entitled *Mini-manual for the Urban Guerrilla.*

Sully put a handkerchief over his nose and grimaced, "Why all the candles, the guy have his electricity shut off?"

"Nope. Utilities are included in the rent he paid Mrs. McGillicuddy. The only thing I can conclude, he preferred candlelight."

The rotting vegetables, mostly cucumbers and zucchini, were in a colander in the kitchen sink, as if the occupant had meant to rinse them and never gotten around to it. The ammoniated stink of urine, which I first assumed was the result of a backed-up toilet, was the first significant indication that Leland Maddock was not merely an indifferent housekeeper, but had been profoundly disturbed.

"Yep," Sheehan said, indicating the multiple rows of glass pint jars neatly stacked in the porcelain bathtub, "he saved all his pee-pee. If you get close enough to look, which I don't recommend, you'll notice he's got the date and time written on the lid of each jar. Also, I found a bunch of articles torn out of medical journals and chemical textbooks, all pertaining to urinalysis. Like maybe old Leland wanted to find out if all the drugs he took showed up in his urine."

"Prescription drugs?" Sully asked, eyeing the medicine cabinet in the tiny bathroom.

"Lots of 'em. Mostly from the Vets Hospital. I got the number of the psychiatrist in charge over there, in case you want to follow up."

Sully said, "Absolutely." He used a pencil to pry open the mirrored cabinet, which proved to be loaded with medication bottles. "This guy was a pill freak. He's got, let me see, uppers, downers, Valium, lithium, Elavil—that's an antidepressant, I think. He's got five brands of aspirin. Also Darvon, muscle relaxants, stomach medicines. Hell, he's even got a bottle of Carter's Little Liver Pills."

Sheehan grinned and said, "Better living through chemistry." He didn't seem to mind the smell. The sergeant was fully aware that locating Leland Maddock's hideaway was an investigative coup, and he was enjoying every minute of the tour. A Lucky Strike appeared at the corner of his mouth, glowing as he inhaled. "I found a couple dozen more bottles in the trash bin," he said, "still sealed. All of it from the outpatient pharmacy at the Vets."

Sully squinted at the cigarette in disapproval, but didn't say anything. In any case, the burning tobacco wasn't proof against the humid stench of the place. Nothing short of fumigation would fix that.

"This way to the boudoir, gentlemen," Sheehan said, gesturing at the open door of a small bedroom.

Like many another vigilant apartment dweller, Leland Maddock kept his firearms in his bedroom closet. He had more than the family shotgun, however. Sheehan gleefully ran down the list.

"Here we have our basic Ruger P-85F. Takes a 9 mm slug. We have our well-known semiauto AK-22, with a state-of-the-art night scope, the AR-15 Sporter—very pricey. We have not one, not two, but three, count them, three, machetes of varying lengths. We have a sawed-off shotgun, 12-gauge, make unknown. In that shoebox are the various pieces of several disassembled small-caliber handguns. He kept his ammo in the footlocker, along with some personal mementos and the key to a safe deposit box."

"He have magnum shells in there?" Sully asked.

"You bet. Same as he was carrying when I made his day. Other thing I noticed about these weapons: most have the serial numbers filed off. My guess is a lot of it is hot. No way could our boy afford these toys on a disability pension."

After determining that Maddock had had access to .44 caliber ammunition, Sully appeared to lose interest in the exotic collection of firearms. He glanced at the newspaper articles in the *Globe* and the *Standard,* mostly light, local-interest angles on the making of the Casey movie that Maddock had kept under his bed, for reasons unknown. He passed them on to me without comment and turned his attention to a green plastic binder he'd found in the footlocker. "You check this out?" he asked Sheehan, hefting the fat scrapbook.

"Haven't had a chance. What's he got in there, dirty pictures?"

"Not exactly," Sully said. He perched on the edge of the ammunition locker, touching down gingerly, and proceeded to polish his glasses with a handkerchief he kept in his breast pocket for that purpose. His manner was deliberate and methodical. He was onto something.

I rolled to his side, aware of the candy wrappers rustling under my wheels. As Sully leafed through the scrapbook he made a low, tuneless whistling sound, like a teapot coming to a boil.

Sheehan leaned over Sully's shoulder, squinting through his cigarette smoke as he peered at the scrapbook. "So what's the big mystery?" he said. "We know Maddock was as crazy as a shithouse rat. Hoarded grocery bags, tin cans, balls of string, candle wax, you name it. Saved his own urine, for that matter. What's the significance of clippings from some crazy magazine?"

"Read it," Sully said.

"Huh?"

"Read the ad."

Sheehan bent lower. The squint, it seemed, was not entirely due to the smoke he was exhaling. "'Soldier of fortune,'" he read, "'seeking danger. All jobs considered. Discretion assured. Reply, *American Mercenary*, Box GH.' Jack, you know anything about a magazine called *American Mercenary*?"

"Not much. A glossy monthly with an emphasis on firearms and conspiracy theories. Published by a retired army general. A gadfly type."

A tight smile played over Sully's face. "They're all the same," he said. "Same wording, with reply to the same box number. And every month that same ad was clipped. Anybody want to take a wager? I'll bet a slice of apple pie that Leland Maddock placed those ads."

"No bet," Sheehan said. He looked around the squalid apartment and shook his head, sucking hard on the Lucky Strike. "Must be a rough life, being a soldier of fortune."

CHAPTER SEVEN

MEGAN MADE NO ATTEMPT TO MASK HER DE-
light at the downpour and the havoc it had caused.
Usually she walks the ten blocks from her office, but that
evening I picked her up outside the Federal-style edifice
of Standish House Publishing on the high end of Beacon
Street, overlooking the Common. A ten-yard dash from
the front door to the van left her soaked to the skin and
laughing.

"Jack," she said, attempting to shake the water from
her hair. "I wish you could have been there. Mary and I
went up to the fifth floor with a pair of binoculars to
watch the show. Bird watching, she called it. They were
filming an exterior shot of this brownstone one block
over, right? It's really a suite of tax lawyers, but for the
movie they made it look like a private residence."

"Right," I said. "That's where Smilin' Stan Seigel
keeps his gun moll mistress."

Meg gave me a doubtful look. "In the book the place
was, I believe, a walk-up in Revere."

"Yeah, well, Lindy wasn't keen on Revere. Said it would photograph bland. So they decided to upgrade the neighborhood."

"I'm glad," she said. "Otherwise we wouldn't have been there to see it. And Mary Kean wouldn't have laughed so hard her bridgework got dislodged. What happened was, they were all set up, right? Lights, cameras, action. Casey is supposed to be leading a SWAT team attack on the building, which is something else I don't remember from the book."

I winced. I'd put the SWAT scene into the script myself, and as far as I knew the scene was being filmed pretty much as I'd written it. No dialogue, just plenty of good old American gunplay. Action and nail-biting suspense, supposedly. Not, as Megan was implying, comedy.

"Okay, the first time they run through it, the timing is off and what's his name, the guy who plays Casey?"

"Burt Bardo."

"Right, how could I forget? So they're out of synch and Bardo gets to the front door too late—he's supposed to be the first inside, I take it?"

"Right," I said. "Exactly."

"Second time, I think it was, one of the extras drops his weapon, the guy behind him trips over it and falls head first into the shrubbery. Keystone Kops couldn't have done it better," Megan said, grinning impishly. "They're setting up to shoot again when it starts to rain. No warning, it just pours down like someone emptied a bucket. The crew goes nuts trying to cover the cameras and lighting equipment. It keeps raining, so they break for coffee, only it's obvious not everyone can fit into the canteen trailer. Quite a few of the lower echelon are left standing out in the rain, casting covetous glances at the trailer. Mary said they looked like a mob getting ready to storm the Bastille."

Mary Kean is my editor, and as such has a proprietary interest in the Casey novels. Indeed, I wouldn't have begun writing them without her encouragement. When the television production company picked up the movie option on *Casey and the Black Widow,* Mary had grinned, clapped her hands together, and said, "Take the money, Jack, have a blast . . . and pay no attention to what happens later. Remember what James Cain said when asked how it felt to have his book ruined by a movie: 'Nobody ruined my book, it's right there on the shelf with every word intact.'"

Mary has a strong, almost profound sense of humor, so I could well imagine how it tickled her to watch the antics of the film crew. Her slightly manic giggle echoed throughout Megan's account of what followed.

"Okay, the rain stops," Meg said, shaping the story with her hands. "Burt Bardo comes out of the trailer, takes his place on the marks, waits for the cue. The shot proceeds. The SWAT team performs flawlessly. Bardo arrives at the front door at exactly the right moment. He has his gun in hand, and even from the fifth floor, a block away, I must say he looked exceedingly debonair and handsome. Okay, he raises the gun, aims at the lock on the door, and fires. The lock explodes on cue. He lifts his right foot and kicks the door open. And then, at exactly that moment, a gutter lets go and about a hundred gallons of cold rainwater drench the poor man, sweeping his perfect little hairpiece off the top of his head and taking it down the steps and out to the street. Where the makeup man made a daring rescue, saving the poor little wig from a fate unknown in the open sewer grate."

"How did Bardo react?"

Megan said, "That's the best part. He had a fit. A

laughing fit. He laughed so hard he was doubled over. And every time they tried to reshoot the scene, he would have *another* laughing fit. He'd get as far as the front door and he'd double over, laughing hysterically. Miss Giddy Bang-Bang was beside herself. Finally she had to give up, call it a day."

By the time Megan finished the anecdote the fickle rain, of course, had stopped, and glimpses of blue sky were visible to the west.

At home we flipped a coin. As a result Meg would stir fry the chicken and I would toss a salad. I checked the answering machine—Lindy Bangs had called twice, sounding faintly hysterical. As requested I returned a call to her room at the Ritz.

To my relief, no one answered.

Pride's Crossing is not, as Meg first assumed, the title of a steamy romance novel. It is a wealthy little neighborhood in Beverly, a Northshore community some thirty miles from Boston. I went to Pride's Crossing on a brisk morning in the second week of September because General George Gritz (U.S. Army, Retired) lived and worked on a big, sprawling estate there.

"It'd be worth the trip just to get a look at the place," Russ White advised me. "That is if you can find a way to see over the twelve-foot concrete wall the general installed a few years back. Locals call it 'the fortress' now. When his father built it—I'm talking about the late Harland Gritz, who invented the Gritz vacuum tube, which is where all the money came from—he spent almost as much on the landscaping as on the buildings. The idea was to make the grounds look like an English country estate. Formal gardens, topiary, water fountains, the works."

"I'm more interested in the general," I said. "Are you

telling me he publishes *American Mercenary* as a hobby?"

I held the receiver away from my ear while Russ chortled. "Just so you don't say it to his face. He considers the magazine a vocation. Writes the editorials himself. Calls his column 'The Gritz World View,' and if you're ever in need of a bizarre conspiracy theory for one of your books, check it out. This is a guy who thinks the Pope had John F. Kennedy killed when he visited the Vatican in 1958."

"Kennedy wasn't assassinated until '63."

"That's your opinion. General Gritz has secret information that the Pope was a hit man for the international Communist-Jewish conspiracy and that he had Kennedy killed and replaced with a double, who was then elected president. That's why the Bay of Pigs failed, because the fake Kennedy was really a Russian agent controlled by the Jewish pope."

"Makes perfect sense," I said. "So will the general talk to me, or is he too busy communing with beings from outer space?"

"Thing of it is, Jack, you'll find him very reasonable in person. Charming as hell. It's only on paper the craziness comes through. I interviewed him when he was pushing for a state referendum to make it a legal requirement that all white males carry a sidearm. Remember that?"

"Now you mention it, yes."

"Well, somehow he made the idea sound reasonable, okay? He's very persuasive. He'll probably talk you into writing 'How to Murder Your Spouse' articles for *American Mercenary*. I hear he pays well."

"From what you say, he can afford to."

"Why the interest in Gritz?" he asked.

"Told you," I said. "I'm doing research for a book."

"Sure you are," Russ said. "Just like I'm going to pitch for the Sox next year."

There were two signs on the heavily fortified gate to the general's estate: HOME OF OLD GLORY PUBLICATIONS and ALL VEHICLES MUST STOP FOR SECURITY CLEARANCE. The young security guard who emerged from the guardhouse, armed with a shoulder-slung M-14 and wearing camouflage fatigues, politely asked me to state my business. I held up a recent issue of *American Mercenary* and said, "I've got an appointment with General Gritz. I called earlier and talked with a Mr. Beaker, his personal secretary."

"*Captain* Beaker," the guard corrected. "Right, let me obtain clearance, please."

He turned smartly and went back to the guardhouse, where he spoke briefly and inaudibly into a telephone. A few moments later he returned with a plastic-embossed pass. "Okay," he said. "You're cleared to park in Lot B. That's adjacent to the East Quad. There are signs, you can't miss it. Leave the pass on the dash, please, and proceed."

The gables and chimneys of the large main building were visible, rising over thick, landscaped foliage that bordered the paved drive. As the guard had implied, the various "quadrants" of the estate and the several parking areas were well marked. There was plenty of room in Lot B, so I saw no problem in taking the space assigned to Gen. George Gritz. If I was going to be saluted, I might as well have a title. The rank of general has appeal, especially when you're a civilian who never got beyond Cub Scout.

The signs directed me to a large, white-shingled stable that had been converted to the use of Old Glory Publications. There were three second-story windows on the gable end. A flag was suspended from each windowsill. A series of bronze plaques on the stable doors further informed me of the various subsidiary operations housed under the same roof: AMERICAN MERCENARY, AMERICAN MERCENARY BOOK CLUB, THE TOTAL WAR SURVIVALIST CATALOGUE.

Pushing my way along the paved path that led to the stable, I concentrated on remembering exactly what lie I'd told Gritz's secretary when setting up the appointment. Considering the general's reputation as a paranoid reactionary, I'd thought it best not to mention my interest in the soldier of fortune ads in the classified section of his magazine, and how they might figure in the attempt on the life of a certain Boston homicide detective.

I also wondered what Sully would think of my subterfuge, and concluded that he would not be pleased.

"Sure I'd like to talk to Gritz," he'd told me. "But I'm out of my jurisdiction out there. I'd have to bring in the local police, or possibly the feds. And just at the moment I'm not in the mood for a party."

Meaning he didn't want Gritz alerted to an ongoing investigation. That's what I was thinking about when I pushed the door bell. A shot rang out. The coincidence was uncanny. I pushed the bell again. Another shot rang out. Weird.

The stable door opened. A short, burly-shouldered man emerged, grinning around a fat green cigar. He wore crisply creased khaki slacks, a Pendleton shirt, and deck shoes. His thick white hair was cut down to short bristles that stood at attention. Eyes an uncanny shade of vinyl blue. He yanked the cigar from his mouth and said, "Last week I had the bell rigged up to *The Ride of the Valkyries*. Which do you think is more effective, Wagner or the retort of a single gunshot?"

He poked the cigar back in his teeth and waited, hands on hips. Clearly I was meant to express an opinion.

"Gunshot," I said after a moment.

The general clapped his hands together and made a thumbs-up. "Right-o," he said, "more bang for the buck. Gritz," he added, extending his right hand. "You're Hawkins. They call you Hawk?"

"Hardly ever," I said, a little surprised to discover that his handshake was gentle. I'd been expecting a bonecrusher.

"Well, Hawk, welcome aboard. I'd offer to push, but you look like a guy can fend for himself."

He held open the door as I wheeled through into a modern office suite. Standard commercial furniture, with an emphasis on teak and chrome. Several young men sat at computer work stations, punching keys and staring earnestly into luminous screens.

"Yessir, I'm happy to be of service. Always admire a writer. Always pay 'em, too. Our free-lancers, I mean. Top rates. Must confess I don't read novels. Nothing against 'em, mind you. No patience. No time. Movies now, I love a good movie."

I expected to see a busy staff laying out the magazine. Gritz explained that the composition and pasteup work was handled by a specialty printer, that the in-house operation was confined to his own editorial duties and to processing the book club and mail order business. The actual warehousing and packaging was done elsewhere.

"Keep it neat and clean, Hawk," he said. "That's the name of the game. I like to think of Old Glory as a think tank. If I let the place get overrun with paster-uppers and ad reps I'd be pestered all day long. Should this go here, what caption, how much per column inch? No, thanks. Can't think clearly in a cluttered atmosphere. Neat and clean, that's the ticket."

Gritz led me briskly through the work station area to the rear part of the stable building. His office, a pine-paneled room overlooking the grounds, was distinctly unmodern by contrast. Emphasis on cracked leather chairs, a modestly scaled oak desk, and a reproduction of a misty American landscape by George Caleb Bingham. On a foggy day, the grounds outside the office window would, I thought, resemble the scene in the painting.

"My adjunct," Gritz said, "Captain Beaker."

Captain Beaker was dressed identically to the general, right down to the comfortably broken-in boat shoes. He was a tall ectomorph of about forty-five. Like his boss, his hair was clipped short, which emphasized the thick, elongated folds of his ears. He had large brown eyes and the earnest, mournful expression of an undertaker looking for business.

"Our pleasure, Mr. Hawkins. Always happy to have a writer drop in," he said without any trace of enthusiasm. After glancing down at a steno pad he added. "Background of a typical American mercenary, I think that was the subject of interest?"

"Right," I said. "I'm working on an adventure novel. One of the characters is a soldier of fortune. Hires out to a foreign government to help engineer a coup."

"Interesting," Beaker said carefully.

"Terrific idea," the general said. He sat on the edge of his desk with his arms folded, puffing the cigar energetically.

"The problem is, I don't know any soldiers of fortune. I was hoping you could give me a profile. What makes a mercenary tick,"

"I like it," the general said. "What makes a mercenary

tick. What are his interests, et cetera. We like to think his interests are what we appeal to in *American Mercenary:* State-of-the-art weaponry. Guerrilla tactics. Up-to-the-minute reports from global hot spots. There are presently—correct me if I'm wrong, Beaker—two hundred and seven separate actions underway worldwide. That is, we *report* on that many. Afghanistan to Zambia."

"That many wars?"

"Warfare is merely another form of human expression," Gritz said amiably. "Tell me, Hawk, you ever been in the military?" he added, glancing at my wheelchair.

"Never had the chance," I said, framing the answer.

Beaker pulled at his long earlobes and looked mournful. General Gritz, in stark contrast, was positively jovial. He said, "For starters, your modern American mercenary typically has a heavy military background. Usually Airborne, Special Services, Navy Seal. The danger boys. Not necessarily a career soldier, mind you. Tends to chaff at military bureaucracy. Highly spirited, action-oriented. Might even say romantic. You agree, Beaker?"

"I do, General."

"He's a man, Hawk, who makes up his own mind. Not opposed to taking orders, of course—respects the chain of command—but prefers to be in charge of his own destiny. A bit of a rebel, authority-wise. Goes without saying, he's willing to put his life on the line." He puffed at the cigar, rolling it from one side of his mouth to the other. "How'm I doing, Beaker?"

"You're doing fine, General."

"This the kind of stuff you need, Hawk?"

"It's a big help, General. Also, I'd like to know how the modern mercenary gets work. I assume he doesn't just sign up for the Foreign Legion."

Gritz liked that. He laughed and slapped his knee. "Not since the French wimped out of the Third World," he said. "Algeria, the Congo, *those* were the days."

"What I was wondering," I said, "suppose I'm just out of the service and I want to hire on as a soldier of fortune. How do I go about it? Is there some kind of international clearinghouse? A worldwide booking agency?"

Gritz shook his head. "Dangerous idea," he said. "Too easy to breach security. No, mostly the hiring gets done underground. Through the grapevine. Who-you-know sort of thing. That fair to say, Beaker?"

"Very fair, sir."

"Suppose," I said, "suppose all his buddies have been killed. He's the only survivor."

"Damned shame," Gritz said with feeling, as if we were discussing an actual person.

"He's all alone in the world and he needs a job," I said, warming to my imaginary character. "He needs to get back into action. What's the first step?"

Gritz nodded thoughtfully. "Tough situation. First thing to do, I recommend your friend find himself a newsstand. Pick up a copy." Gritz held up the latest issue of *American Mercenary*. The cover was a dark jungle scene with a crouching Asian soldier illuminated by the red spotlight of a night scope. "Read it," Gritz advised, "cover to cover. Absorb the information. Get a feel for the market, the strategies for getting hired. Then flip to the classifieds."

I was careful not to look surprised or pleased that the subject had been raised. "Classifieds?" I asked.

"We think of it as a global billboard. Say you're a member of a small Third World government, looking to undertake a coup. Naturally you want to do it right. You check under the Expert Consultant heading. There it is: 'Strategy consultant, coup management, specializing in small tactical actions.' Or say, like your hard-luck friend, he looks under Free-lance.' He'd find 'Wanted: combat instructors, equatorial terrain, expertise in explosives & covert night-ops preferred. Salary negotiable.'"

"So he could put an ad in there himself, stating his experience, and you'd forward any replies?"

"Sure. Like I say, it's a kind of global billboard. You might even call it a dating service, eh, Beaker?"

"Indeed, sir," the captain said in a mournful tone, "you might."

She walked through the rain, welcoming the torrents. Let it rain until the floodwaters rose, until all the living world was submerged, and the earth was clean again.

Ahead of her the vine-covered parapets of the church glistened. This had once been her refuge. No longer. And yet there was one inside, behind the dark screen, who would listen.

She entered by the side door and knelt. A puddle of rainwater formed at her knees. She muttered, communing with her Voices, and then moved to the confessional.

Behind the screen a discreet cough.

"Teresa, I asked you not to come here."

She said: "Would you deny me?"

There was a long silence before he answered. "No. I cannot. But please, Teresa, do not speak of blasphemy. Remember you are in a holy place."

She wove her fingers into the screen and clung to it.

"This is my confession. God has sinned against me. He has taken my name in vain. He has condemned my husband to hell, and loosed the voices of angels in my head."

The priest sighed. "God forgives you," he said.

"Yes! Yes!" She pressed her lips to the screen and shouted. "But do I forgive Him? Do I, Father? Ask the Voices. Ask the itchy things inside my head."

He made soothing noises. She, in her madness, wept.

CHAPTER EIGHT

IT WAS RAINING WHEN I LEFT OLD GLORY ES-
tates. It was raining so hard I expected to see fish
swimming by the windshield. I wondered how Lindy
Bangs and her film crew were faring, and if they'd found
waterproof glue for Burt Bardo's hairpiece.

I wondered if George Gritz was aware that his magazine had been providing a service for hired assassins, as
well as for soldiers of fortune. I wondered if he saw a
distinction between the two occupations. I wondered
what made Captain Beaker look so sad. I wondered who
had hired Leland Maddock to kill Tim Sullivan, and
why.

I wondered who, who wrote the book of love.

That riff from the golden oldie was running through
my head as I concentrated on locating Route 128 through
the driving rain. Maybe Route 128 had been eroded
away by the deluge, because I never did find it, and

drove most of the way back to Boston along the curving coast, through the witch town of Salem and yacht-cluttered Marblehead, eventually picking up the highway again in Saugus, where giant plastic dinosaurs grazed silently in the rain, apparently undeterred by the proliferation of franchised hamburgers and waterbed motels.

At home there were three calls on the machine. The first two were from Lindy Bangs. I dialed her room at the Ritz and was surprised when she answered on the first ring.

"Lindy," I said. "Jack Hawkins."

"Jack, ooh, I'm so bummed I could cry. In fact I *am* crying."

I asked what was wrong.

"It's *raining*, Jack. Can't shoot exteriors in the rain. Production says we have to go into delay. They've put the crew on standby until the weather clears. So I'm over budget and Burt fucking Bardo is scheduled to start a feature film the second week in October. In *Hong Kong* of all places."

I wasn't sure how to respond. Did she want a sympathetic ear, a shoulder to cry on, or an opinion from a meteorologist?

"Screw the weatherman," she said. "I've had it with weathermen. What I had in mind, I thought maybe you'd like to come over and keep me company. I'm on my lonesome here."

"Love to," I said. "except I've got this 4:30 appointment with my attorney."

She sighed. It was a great big sigh, and left a lot of room for whatever I might want to imagine. "Know what Shakespeare said about lawyers? 'Kill all the lawyers,' that's what he said."

"I'll mention that to mine," I said. "I'm sure he'll have an opinion."

*　　*　　*

Fitzy was waiting at Vincent's, a Comm Ave bistro he favors because of the free happy-hour buffet. When I rolled in he looked up from an overloaded plate and said, "I recommend the bean dip. We're talking major garlic. Exhale this stuff at the Atheneum and you'd clear the room faster than a bomb threat."

Finian X. Fitzgerald and I go way back. We cut classes together at St. Luke's, faked our way through Latin High, dated the same girls without coming to blows, quite. After four years as B.U. day students we parted ways, temporarily: Fitzy bartended nights to get through law school and I got married to my college sweetheart, Marge, and settled into a civil service job with the Boston Police Department. Fitzy and Marge were mutually repelled, which put some stress cracks in the friendship, but it didn't prevent me from being best man when he and Lois got hitched, or godfather to their twins. It didn't prevent Fitzy from winning me a monster award from the city when a screw-loose cop put a bullet in my spine, or from handling my divorce when Marge wanted to bail out.

I tend to think of him as a lithesome, athletic kid with a mop of wiry red hair and a ready grin. Of late he's widened considerably around the hips and his freckled scalp is clearly visible through his thinning hair, but in the nonphysical essentials he's unchanged. He's still generous to a fault and he still loves to hear himself talk.

"So yesterday I'm up on the hill," he began, meaning the state house, "doing my damnedest to convince our fine body of lawmakers they should assist the Coalition of Neighborhood Associations by passing a certain piece of legislation, when who puts the arm on me but the commissioner's butt boy, Liam Delaney."

"The Weasel?"

"None other. He's up there making sure everyone knows the police commissioner's position on the bill, which is, I believe, down on all fours and feeding from the same trough as the rest of the duly appointed piglets. This is the same Liam Delaney who before he got the job thought that public relations were why whores got arrested. A guy with eyes like the marbles we used to kick around the yard at St. Luke's." Fitzy paused to crunch his way through a taco shell and wash it down with a slug of beer. "It was his own mother, I believe, who started calling him Weasel," he added.

"I'm beginning to think you've got a crush on him."

"I especially love the purple carbuncle on his nose. It's bright enough to read by. Anyhow, I'm in the lobby there and Liam sidles up to me. You know, like a cottonmouth sidles up to a bullfrog? He gives me the usual rap about how I ought to quit representing low-rent nonprofits such as CONA and sign up with right-minded organizations like the Police Union and the Teamsters. Long and short of it, he wants to buy me a drink."

"The Weasel? Come on."

"Hey, I was stunned. Guy hasn't paid for anything that passed his lips since his sister frenched him for a nickel. Anyhow, we go over to the Bull where, it so happens, the commissioner has a tab. So it's the taxpayers who pay for my drink, not Liam, and right away I feel better, not being indebted to that slimeball."

"What did he want?"

"Wanted to impart a little information. Having to do with Sully, if you can believe the Weasel. Which I tend not to. Guy could lie his way past St. Peter. Anyhow, he's got this long story about how the Calvino brothers are getting spooked by the grand jury that's been hearing evidence for it seems like the last few decades. What they're bothered about he can't say exactly. I tell him, I say to him, 'Liam, there's been at least one Calvino brother either under indictment or in prison since Eisenhower was copping Z's at the White House. What's the big deal about this particular grand jury?' So he gives me that sideways look. Like he's got a great big secret he can't share, on penalty of death. 'I'm not at liberty to say. What pertains here is that the word on the street is that Detective Sullivan has offended someone in the Lenny Calvino family. I was hoping you could apprise Sully of that, outside of normal channels.'"

"He really talk like that, Fitz?"

Fitzy held up his right hand, palm out. "Scout's honor," he said. "Liam has a special fondness for the phrase 'what pertains here.' I ask him point blank exactly who has it in for Sully, and why. He starts blinking, like I put something in his eye. Blink, blink. I'm thinking maybe it's a secret code, he's spelling it out with his fat little eyelids. Finally he lowers his voice—big husky whisper—he says, 'According to my intelligence, it is not Fat Lenny himself, but someone connected to his immediate family. In other words, Detective Sullivan's offense is not a business matter, but a personal affront of some sort.' I say to him, I say, 'Come on Liam, are you telling me the attempt on Sully's life was a mob hit? All I know is what I read in the papers, but it sure doesn't *look* like a mob hit. This nutball Leland Maddock wasn't connected to the mob. He was barely connected to the planet Earth.'"

"Fitzy," I said. "Did Liam say anything about a woman?"

He shook his head. "The bastard was entirely evasive. The message he wanted me to deliver—outside of channels, he kept stressing that—was that Fat Lenny is so busy fending off the grand jury that he can't take care of family business."

"Implying that Fat Lenny didn't approve of the hit and is taking steps to correct the situation?"

"That was the general impression. What I kept thinking, all the time Liam is yapping at me, is why information from a mobster like Calvino is coming to me through the police commissioner's deputy in charge of public relations. Kind of makes you wonder, don't it?"

I crunched a taco chip. "You're right about the bean dip," I said. "Garlic *fortissimo.*"

Lindy Bangs was curled up on a king-size bed, stroking a pregnant blue-eyed cat named George. Her eyes were red, the result of an allergy to cat hair. Or so she claimed.

"My heart loves cats and my body hates them," she said. "So what does that say about me?"

"Lindy, if the concierge finds out you've got an animal in here, *he'll* be the one having kittens."

She made a shushing noise. "Not in front of George. George speaks only Siamese, but she understands English perfectly."

"You seem to be taking it well enough, the rain delay."

"Don't be fooled by the package," she said. "I'm a wreck."

Hers was a lovely, red-haired package in a short silk wrap that showed a lot of very shapely leg. She said, "It could be worse. We have most of the interior shots in the can, so it's too late to cancel. They'll just have to live with the extra expense. And if, heaven forbid, it rains for the next three weeks, we'll have to shoot around Bardo, or use a double."

"Or rewrite."

"Sure," she said with languorous enthusiasm, "we could do that."

"It'll all work out."

"Meanwhile, back at the Ritz." Lindy rolled over on the big bed, flopping her arms out. George purred. "I called down and asked if they had anything to cheer up a very dreary evening. They suggested champagne. What do you recommend?"

"I can't argue with champagne."

"Oh good," she said. "Pop the cork and pour. You know what I'd really like? I'd like you to stay for dinner. I'll call down for something fabulous."

That was how I got seriously in dutch with Megan, who had supper in the oven and fire in her eye when at last I made it home, smelling of effervescent wine and the perfume Lindy Bangs had playfully sprayed from an atomizer, to lessen the scent of cat. Or so she claimed.

At first the butcher did not see her. She was dressed all in black, the way they used to do in the old country, and she moved furtively. A shoplifter, a thief? He looked but could not see her eyes. Hidden under the brim of an ancient, ragged hat. The kind long out of fashion.

"Whatta you want, lady?" he asked.

She approached the counter and then he could see her eyes. She was covered from head to toe but her eyes were naked. Gleaming with somber emptiness. The butcher, who could not abide pain, looked away.

"I need blood," she said.

"Excuse me?"

"Blood."

The butcher was uneasy. Casually he backed away from the counter, putting more distance between himself and the woman with the naked eyes. "Lady, you need blood, maybe you should go to the hospital, see a doctor."

Her white hands crawled along the edge of the counter,

as if her fingers had a life of their own. "Calf's blood," she said.

It clicked for the butcher. The woman in black was spooky, no doubt about that, but quite a few of the old-country types used calf's blood for sausage. The request was fairly rare nowadays, but it was not unreasonable. The strangeness in her eyes had fooled him.

"How much do you want?" he asked.

She reached into the fold of her black dress and held up a glass mason jar.

"Enough to fill this."

CHAPTER NINE

THESE WERE THE ITEMS OF INTEREST IN
Leland Maddock's safe deposit box:

    1. twenty-five hundred dollars in cash;

    2. a path lab report;

    3. a clipping from a *Boston Standard* article that mentioned Tim Sullivan in relation to the Casey movie;

    4. a picture torn from an old issue of *Ring* magazine.

The cash was in well-circulated twenties, the lab report was negative, stating that the "urine sample reveals no trace of metallic substance," the article about Sullivan was by Russ White, and the *Ring* picture was of Tony Torelli, a heavyweight boxer.

"Kid Tony," Sheehan said. "Remember him? Local pug makes good. He was big news in the North End for a couple years until Marciano decked'm in the first round of an exhibition match. Now he's ancient history. Last I ever heard of Kid Tony he was pushing a broom for the parish priest."

"Metallic substance," I said, turning to Sully. "What was Maddock looking for, poison?"

Sully ignored the question and read from the *Standard* article. "'A lifelong Jamaica Plain resident, Detective Sullivan is considered one of the best investigators in the elite Homicide Unit, and as such is reputed to be the inspiration for Casey, the popular detective-hero created by author J. D. Hawkins.' That son of a bitch reporter gave out my address. Right in the newspaper."

"Not your street address," I said. "Just your neighborhood."

"Yeah? I notice he doesn't mention where *you* live."

"I was hoping for more," Sheehan said, indicating the evidence package, in this case a shoebox. "A written confession would have been nice. Or a diary."

We were in Sullivan's office at the Berkeley Street Police Headquarters. Sully had requested my presence for reasons not entirely clear to me. The implication, however, was that I was somehow to blame for him having been the focus of murderous attention. An onus I could not, in good conscience, completely ignore.

"No names, no numbers, no receipts," Sheehan lamented. He fingered the pile of bills. "This could be his life savings, for all we know."

"It's half of a nice round number," I said.

"So?" The old belligerence crept back into Sheehan's nasal voice, reminding me that he was a Chelsea tough, and I wasn't.

"Five thousand," I said agreeably. "Maybe that's the going rate for a soldier of fortune. Half as a down payment, remainder on satisfactory completion of the job."

"Only he got fired," Sheehan smirked.

"What do you think?" I asked Sully, directing the theory to him. "Five grand sound right for a murder?"

"More than sufficient," he said, staring into an empty coffee mug, as if looking for clues in the grounds. "There are sadistic punks who'd do it gratis, just to make a good impression with a certain bloated businessman."

He meant Fat Lenny Calvino. I'd expected him to scoff at the rumor passed from Liam Delaney, through Fitzy, to me. Instead his reaction had been puzzled: Why hadn't Delaney contacted him directly? What game was the Weasel playing? Clearly the report troubled him.

"I don't know Fat Lenny," he mused. "I don't know anyone in his 'family.' I've never investigated a Calvino-related homicide. The whole idea of this being a mob thing is nuts."

"Delaney is tryin' to psych you out for some reason," Sheehan said. "Fat Lenny, if he wanted you whacked out, I hate to say it but you'da been whacked. There wouldn'ta been nothin' fancy like car bombs, or disguises. Just good old-fashioned Sicilian firepower."

"Thanks, Larry."

"All I'm sayin', Lieutenant, I sincerely don't think you have to worry about that fat fuck Calvino. Way I see it, with Maddock out of the picture, your troubles are over."

Larry Sheehan didn't have to wait long to find out that trouble was far from over. Just as I was getting ready to leave, Marilyn came in with the morning mail: circulars, magazines, departmental memos, and a small package done up in adhesive tape and brown paper. She put it all in the tray on Sully's desk and asked him if he needed a glass of water to wash down the aspirin he was about to swallow.

He shook his head no, and then spotted the package. "What's that?" he said.

Sheehan caught on immediately. He gingerly hefted

the package. "Got your name on it, and it's heavy," he said, returning it gently to the mail tray. "Let's get out of here."

Sully, using the intercom on Marilyn's desk, ordered the floor cleared. The bomb squad arrived about fifteen minutes later. While they set up their portable blast bunkers, Sully paced the hall one floor below and polished his glasses until the lenses appeared to vanish. He had one instruction for the sergeant who commanded the squad.

"Don't destroy the package."

"The procedure we like to follow, sir, is we—"

"Don't destroy the package."

As it happened, there was no need to detonate the package. It did not contain an explosive device. What it did contain made a lot less sense than a bomb. The squad sergeant, still wearing his heavily padded flak jacket, came down to report the discovery of one mason jar, contents unknown.

"A jar? What's in it?"

"You better have a looksee yourself, Lieutenant."

The mason jar was perched on the sandbag where it had been carefully unwrapped by the sergeant, using extended tongs through a slit in the barricade. The shredded paper wrapping lay in a little heap, like brown confetti.

"Jesus," Sheehan said. "I hope that ain't what I think it is."

It was a quart canning jar, manufactured by the Ball Jar Company, and it was full to the brim with a dark red liquid. Something thin and black and solid lay coiled against the inside, obscured by the opaque contents.

"Get Forensics up here," Sully said. He didn't wait for the lab boys, however. Using his white hanky to get a good grip, he cracked the seal on the lid. A rich, coppery odor instantly pervaded the room.

"Blood," Sheehan muttered. "This is getting weird."

It was going to get a lot weirder. Sully got a plastic ruler out of his desk and fished around inside the jar, snagging whatever it was that lay coiled inside and lifting it out of the thick, clotting liquid.

As the blood dripped away I saw a string of black rosary beads, with a small black crucifix attached.

Sheehan said, "Jesus Christ."

Hugh Devlin, the *Standard* publisher, likes to break a major story on Sunday, when the circulation is at its highest. Megan and I were seated at the kitchen table when she noticed the headline. I'd put together a late breakfast of fresh-squeezed orange juice, sliced melon, sausage links, and pancakes that were precisely as thick as the blueberries inside. The treat was in the nature of a heartfelt bribe.

"For three days I have suffered," I said as she hid behind the paper. "Notwithstanding the fact that I apologized for coming home late smelling of champagne—"

"And perfume. Don't forget the perfume."

"—and for the rudeness of not calling when for all you knew I might have been kidnapped by extraterrestrials—"

The newspaper snapped. "I'd call it a close encounter, buster."

"In demonstrating the deep profundity of my love for you, I sent you flowers at work. A rose on the hour, every hour—"

"A cheap trick."

"Anything but cheap, believe me. I bought you an equally expensive perfume and offered to let you spray me with it, thus establishing territorial rights to my person—"

The newspaper snapped again. "Very funny."

"And lastest but not leastest, I crawled on my elbows to the wilds of eastern Maine and picked a pint of perfect blueberries for you, only you."

"That's a lie. It's also ungrammatical."

"I give up."

"Jack," Meg said, her voice no longer bantering. "You see this?"

She held up the page and tapped a fingernail under the headline.

COP FLICK CAUGHT IN CROSSFIRE

ATTEMPTED MURDER, BLOOD, BOMB THREATS SCARE OFF FILM CREW

I got as far as the end of the second paragraph, saw that it was attributed to an "unnamed source," and reached for the telephone. It rang before I could pick up the receiver.

"About the story—" Sully began in a tight, angry voice.

"Just saw it. About to call Russ White. I am not, repeat not, the source."

Sullivan hung up and I punched Russ's unlisted home phone number.

"You're calling to give me hell," he answered affably. "Fire away."

"Russ, you might at least have warned me. It's taken me five years to reestablish a minimal level of credibility with the Boston Police Department. Credibility which is now blown."

"You're not the source, buddy boy."

"Nobody is going to believe that. And if it's true, who the hell *is* your source?"

"A little birdy."

"Be that way then. And what's this reference to a 'gallon of human blood'? If your little birdy is reliable, you know it was a quart of calf's blood."

"Devlin's twist. There'll be a correction to the follow-up in tomorrow's edition."

"And this stuff about the film crew getting freaked by bomb threats," I said, skimming the article as I talked. "That's bull. It's a rain delay. Inclement weather. The director said so."

"Talk to the production manager. A Mr. Clarence Higgs of B-Line Productions. I'll give you his number, if you don't believe me. According to Higgs there have been bomb threats. Repeated threats by telephone and through the mail. Wording of said threats similar to those attributed to unknown female who threatened Sullivan prior to the attempt on his life. The film company is worried about liability. The rain was a good excuse to hold up production until they can sort it out."

"Shit." In a weak moment I let myself imagine I had the use of my legs back, so I could kick Lindy Bangs a good one right on her pretty little derriere.

"You gotta admit," Russ was saying. "The crucifix floating in blood is pretty spooky."

"It wasn't floating." I skimmed through to the end of the article as Meg watched me with an expression of concern. "Okay, assuming you're correct about the movie delay, where did you get this about Sully being stalked by a band of mercenaries? And why bring General Gritz into it? Hell, he'll sue your ass off."

"Not my department," Russ said. He slurped at what I assumed was coffee, unless he'd gotten into morning nips. "Sullivan was definitely stalked by at least one mercenary, the late Leland Maddock, and if you'll read the paragraph carefully that's exactly what I said. I go on to say there is *conjecture* in the department that other hired guns may be involved."

"Your birdy tell you that?"

"The same. As to Gritz, he's already hip deep in alligators. Four murders-for-hire have been traced to professional killers advertising in his classified section. The feds have been looking into it for more than a year. There's reason to believe he may be liable, if not in criminal than in civil court. Which is exactly what I state in the article."

The air was rapidly exiting my angry red balloon, but there was enough left to bid Russ a curt good-bye. I punched Sully's number and devoted twenty minutes to convincing him I was not ratting to the newspapers, and that although Russ White was a friend I had no control over what he or the *Standard* published.

"Maybe you should look at it this way," I said, concluding my arguments. "If there is a contract out on you, all the publicity is bound to make them gun-shy. Calvino is in trouble enough already without being suspected of a cop killing."

Sully's response was tired, wooden. "It's not Calvino," he said.

"Yeah? Then who is it?"

He said, "I'll handle it."

The place smelled of charred wood and dampness and the cloying scent of candles. They knelt before her makeshift altar. Teresa and her gentle giant. The mercenary had failed. This time she would need cunning, and she would need help.

She held his scarred, clumsy hands. Huge broken fists.

"You must do this thing for me," she whispered, using the old language. "God commands it."

A small sound came from deep in his throat.

"You must," she urged. "The Voices have spoken. The angels are waiting. Can you hear them fluttering? Can you hear the rush of wings?"

The small sound became a whimper. He nodded.

"Good," she said. "This is what you must do."

CHAPTER TEN

IT WAS NEVER CLEAR EXACTLY WHEN TIM
Sullivan disappeared. At some point between Sunday afternoon and Monday morning his friends and co-workers
lost contact with him. His secretary Marilyn was the first
to voice concern when he did not report or call in by 8:00
A.M. on Monday, as was his habit. Her attempt to reach
him by telephone was unsuccessful. His beeper was acti-
vated, but he did not respond. Messages relayed through
the Turret and broadcast over the car radio system were
similarly unproductive.

At 9:15 A.M. Sergeant Detective Lawrence Sheehan
arrived at Sullivan's home and reported that his car,
newly supplied by the motor pool, was not there, and
that the doors to his house and attached garage were
locked. Sheehan gained entry—he never explained
how—and determined that Sully was not inside, nor was
there any indication of an unusual event, as Sheehan put
it—in other words, no sign of violence or abduction.

I learned some of this when Marilyn called an hour

before noon and asked in a shaky, strained voice if I'd seen Sully, or heard from him, or could shed light on where he might be found.

"Marilyn, what's wrong?"

She sniffed back tears. I was stunned—this was a woman with a very tight rein on her emotions. Even when Sully had been gravely injured she'd carried on in a steadfast manner. "I've got a real bad feeling on this one, Jack," she said. "Something awful has happened."

I have no great regard for the powers of extrasensory perception, but knowing Marilyn's rational, businesslike approach to life, her sudden intuition was chilling.

"I assume there's an APB out on him?"

"Yes. Every officer in the unit is out on the street. The chief has put out a department-wide directive. First priority is to find his sedan, taking it street by street. Meantime Larry's on his way to the North End to see Mr. Calvino."

I did a few spin jobs around the apartment to let off nervous energy, my thoughts whirling faster than my wheels. The last thing I'd said to Sully was not to worry. His clipped response indicated that he had a specific suspect in mind, and intended to do something about it.

I'll handle it, he'd said.

If not Calvino or his henchmen, then who? The crazy-sounding woman who had been calling to complain about voices coming from her switched-off TV set? A woman with, as Sully described it, "a shivering kind of laugh?" A woman who had, in her persistent, maddening way, once called at three in the morning to tell him he had a sacred heart?

I thought of the rosary beads immersed in the jar of blood and tried to fathom the possible significance. Was it a symbol of some deranged theology, a hallucinatory nightmare religion? Had Sully, with his Jesuit education, gotten some message or clue from the blood and the beads that remained obscure to heathens like myself?

Was he out there somewhere, caught up in the throes of an investigation, or had he been taken?

I pushed harder, circumnavigating the living room, my wheels squealing on the turns. The apartment was closing in on me. I had to get out. I had to do something.

Larry Sheehan was paying a visit to Fat Lenny Calvino. That left only one other name to try—and that was a longshot at best.

The North End is one of the few neighborhoods in Boston that has remained essentially intact over the last few decades. There have been incursions on the flanks, and the wharves have been taken over by slick real-estate speculators, but the core area enclosed by Commercial Street and the southeast expressway is still heavily Italian. The narrow, winding streets and corner cafés look Italian, smell Italian, sound Italian. The language lives here. And though the Irish dominate the political structure of the city, and the cops, and the Archdiocese, I was not at all surprised to find that the pastor of St. Anthony's was one Father Francesco Fabrizzi, a Neapolitan by birth. After bullying my way past his elderly housekeeper, who regarded me with deep suspicion, I found him in the ground-floor office, going over the parish ledgers.

Father Fabrizzi was a small, boyish-looking man with jet black hair. He had pale, translucent skin that looked steely blue where he'd shaved close, and clear brown eyes that regarded me thoughtfully after hearing my declaration that I had to see him on an emergency basis, as a matter of life or death.

"Who is dying?" he asked, getting up from his desk.

"No one, I hope." I went on to explain that my friend,

a police detective, was missing. "It's possible he came here to interview someone who works for your parish."

That elicited a raised eyebrow. "I myself was in our little church for most of the day, of course," the priest explained. "If we had a visitor here at the rectory it would have been mentioned, I think. Who was it your friend the detective wanted to see?"

"Tony Torelli."

The priest smiled. He appeared relieved, as if he had been expecting me to name someone else. "Ah, yes," he said. "Our gentle giant, Antonio. Tell me, does this detective know Antonio?"

"No," I said, "His name came up in connection with an investigation."

Father Fabrizzi nodded and spread his hands, palms upward. "I say this because Antonio would not make, I think, a suitable interview."

"Why is that?"

"If you like, you shall see for yourself. Come, we shall find him in the garden, I think."

I followed the priest through the dark hallways of the rectory. We emerged into a small courtyard bordered on one side by the church building, and enclosed by a high, vine-covered brick wall. The city was all around us, but invisible under a wet gray sky, and it pleased me to think it would not be so very different in any church courtyard in Naples. There was a pear tree and a small grape arbor and a stone bench upon which a fat blue pigeon strutted. Sprawling tomato plants, heavy with ripening fruit, were fixed to a row of rough wooden stakes.

A large man crouched by the plants, his back to us. His shoulders were wide and powerful and the cords of his neck stood out like steel cables as he worked his hands through the earth, pulling weeds.

Father Fabrizzi spoke quietly. "You know that Antonio was once a prizefighter?"

"Yes," I said. "A heavyweight."

"There were, I have been told, many blows to the head. This happened many years ago, but there was some damage to the brain. You will find that he understands what you say, but it is difficult for him to form words."

When the priest called his name Kid Tony stood up and turned slowly around, facing us. His big, scarred hands were stained brown with the rich dirt of the garden. Despite the loose, striped coveralls he looked like some kind of huge, primeval farmer. A Cro-Magnon gardener with a broad, dented forehead and hair the color and consistency of steel wool. The old boxer's face was a jumble of planes divided by scars, as if it had once been chopped apart and never quite reassembled. You could see where his nose had been broken and then broken again, until it was little more than a lump of flesh between dark, bloodshot eyes that were not so much empty as extraordinarily quiet.

"Antonio, this gentleman would like to speak with you."

I took two snapshots from my shirt pocket and held one out to the former heavyweight. He looked impassively at Father Fabrizzi. When the priest nodded, Torelli took the snapshot from my hand.

"The man in the picture is a good friend of mine," I said. "We think he's in trouble and we're trying to find him. Did he come here to see you, Tony?"

The big man looked at the picture for what seemed an unusually long time. The dark, quiet eyes glanced at me, then away, and he shook his head.

I said, "He's a policeman, Tony. His name is Detective Sullivan. Someone is trying to hurt him. They may be hurting him right now. Are you sure he never came here and asked you questions?"

He held the snapshot closer. His lower lip slowly jutted out. Tendons pulsed in the side of his jaw as he concentrated. Then, slowly and firmly, he shook his head again.

"No come here," he said. His voice was like gravel sliding down a chute.

I gave him the other snapshot.

"This man's name was Leland Maddock. He may have used other names. Do you know him?"

Torelli studied the morgue shot. He started to smile and I assumed he was going to indicate that he knew Maddock. Then I realized he was unconsciously mimicking the rictus grin in the picture.

"Maddock spent time in the Veterans Hospital," I explained to the priest. "I thought it possible Tony might have met him there, or as an outpatient."

Father Fabrizzi nodded, and touched a hand to the boxer's shoulder. "Where you ever a soldier, Antonio?"

Torelli shook his head, handing the snapshot back to me. "No fight," he said. "No fight." Then he turned his broad back to us and returned to the garden, running his broken hands through the earth.

The priest showed me out through a side gate. He paused at the gate. I could see the question forming even as he struggled to find the proper words.

"Is this friend, your policeman," he said, "he is the one in the newspaper yesterday? The sacrilege with the animal blood and the rosary beads?"

I nodded. "I don't know what the blood business meant, if anything, but Sully may be in trouble with a person who lives in this neighborhood. Do you know who the Calvinos are, Father?"

The priest nodded. "Of course. Everyone knows them here. You might say that Mr. Calvino, the fat one, he is my only misfortune since I come here."

"Why is that?"

Father Fabrizzi sighed, loosening the starched collar at his neck. "He belongs to this parish, you see. Last year his daughter got married here. Nice enough girl, but her father is, you will pardon me, a pig of a man. He slaps me on the back so hard I fall down, almost. And the cursing! Right in the vestry, before the ceremony, he takes the name in vain in the most filthy way. When he sees that I am offended he laughs and makes another filthy jest about Naples and those who were born there. I think he hates all Neapolitans, this Calvino. Perhaps he hates all human beings."

"Does Tony know Fat Lenny?"

The priest shrugged, using his whole body. "Here, *everyone* knows him. They do not let you forget."

"They?"

"The Calvino soldiers. The men on the street corners, you have seen them, smoking their little cigars and wearing the dark glasses. They stand around and talk and smoke and appear to do nothing with their lives. Some are involved in gambling, others drugs, still more buy and sell stolen merchandise. Some, I am told, peddle vile pictures of little children—pornography—not here in the neighborhood, but in stores downtown. So how can anyone forget Calvino? He is everywhere, you will pardon me please, like shit in a sewer." He paused and cleared his throat. "I hope I have not offended."

"No, Father, not at all," I said. "One last question. We think there's a woman involved. A crazy sounding woman who threatened Lieutenant Sullivan over the phone. Rumor has it that she's connected to the Calvino's, that she has something against cops. Something worth killing for. Does that ring any bells?"

He looked away, as if searching for a thought, or the husk of memory, then shook his head. "I have not heard this rumor," he said. He offered me his hand. "Now I must go back to my ledgers. Columns of figures; sometimes I think they become as important to us as the true work of the church."

The van was parked several blocks away. Pushing my way slowly through the quiet, modest neighborhood of fruit markets and candy stores, I found it difficult to comprehend how those few dozen blocks generated the quantity of money that was needed to keep the Calvino machine functioning. To all appearances it was a bricked-up world of blacktop lawns, shabby tenements, and dissolute dreams. The kind of place where only a cockroach or a bloodsucker could get fat.

What had Sully stumbled on here that had put him in jeopardy? What had he learned or seen that prompted at least two attempts on his life by a killer-for-hire?

As one with a professional interest in the criminal underworld, I well knew it was almost unheard of for a gangland boss to undertake the murder of a city police detective. Fat Lenny Calvino was unlikely to make such a dangerous move unless his motive was extraordinarily compelling. Jealousy over a mistress or family member would not suffice, despite the rumors Liam Delaney was floating. Even damaging testimony from Sully would not be reason enough, not with the army of wily attorneys Calvino had at his disposal, who had been defending him against grand juries, federal probes, and racketeering charges for most of his adult life. Calvino was a convenient focus of attention, but without evidence to the contrary I could not believe he was directly responsible for Tim Sullivan's disappearance.

If Sully's problem originated in the North End, it had to be something out of the mainstream of the criminal enterprise Calvino controlled. A loose cannon in the neighborhood, someone not directly under the thumb of the gangland boss. Someone who needed to go outside to hire a killer, rather than through the established channels.

I stopped at a corner market and bought an apple from one of the stalls. Two bits for a fresh Macintosh picked by Jamaicans in New Hampshire and sold by Italians in an Irish city in North America. Maybe it was the rich ethnicity that made it taste so sharp and sweet.

The New Hampshire part reminded me that the bucolic, tax-free state to the north was a favorite dumping ground for gangland slayings. The time-honored method, which caused jurisdictional nightmares for Boston investigators, usually involved an abandoned vehicle with a bullet-riddled body in the trunk.

The apple went sour in my mouth. Maybe that's why I was so resistant to the idea of Calvino being responsible for Sully's trouble—because the final scene would take place on a road in the New Hampshire marshlands, in the awful, airless silence of a trunk.

I tossed the apple in a litter basket and pushed my way over the rutted sidewalks toward my van. Heading for home.

On my left, boarded up and apparently abandoned, was the burned-out shell of a small church. The spire and most of the main roof were gone. All that remained were the walls and the stone vaults and a rusted iron fence that enclosed the property.

I wouldn't have given the place a second look except for the fact that a large figure emerged from under the arch of the boarded-up doorway. As he moved from the shadows of the ruin a slant of light struck his broad shoulders and massive head. Despite the dramatic lighting, it was not a biblical figure who blocked my way on the sidewalk, but the former heavyweight, Kid Tony Torelli.

He stopped a yard in front of me with his big hands loose at his sides. His throat worked. A word emerged from his scarred lips.

"My friend," he said. "You know my friend?"

"Who?"

"Cop friend."

Clearly the old boxer had followed me to ask the question without being overheard by the priest who employed him. I had no idea who he was talking about, but for a moment hope flared. "Is this cop friend Detective Sullivan?" I asked. "You might know him as Tim, or Sully."

He blinked eyes as dark and dull as bits of coal, and shook his head.

"Does he have a name, this cop pal of yours? Where can I find him?"

Kid Tony stared at the ground and mumbled something. I rolled closer.

"My friend dead," he said, as if just recalling the fact. "Gone to Heaven."

This was getting nowhere. Too many blows to the head had left him permanently punch drunk, unable to sustain a train of thought, or even to remember who was living, who was dead.

"Sorry," I said. "But I've got a missing friend, too. Maybe we should get together, go ask Fat Lenny. Maybe *he* knows what happens to missing friends, hey Tony?"

He answered by walking away. He loped through the iron-fenced yard like an old, wounded panther, disappearing into the shadows of the ruined church. Leaving me alone on the mean streets, in a place I did not know, on turf that was not mine.

CHAPTER ELEVEN

I WAS HAVING MY MORNING BLAST OF OJ when Larry Sheehan called with the news that Sully's car had been recovered.

"Great," I said. "Where'd he leave it?"

"No idea," Sheehan said. His voice sounded phlegmy, muffled.

"I thought you said you'd found the car?"

"Right. Over here in Somerville, in a dirt lot near the tracks."

"Somerville?" I said, confused. "Sully was in Somerville?"

"Like I said," Sheehan snapped, exasperated. "I got no idea if he came to Somerville. The car was stripped, get it?"

"Sorry," I said.

"You dumb fuck, it was *stolen*, okay? Taken out here and then stripped. Must be fifty stripped vehicles nearby. So it tells us nothing, get it? Wherever Sully left his car it got ripped off. Might have been from his driveway, might have been the waterfront, coulda been anywhere in Greater Boston."

"Oh," I said.

"Good news is, no sign of foul play. Whatever happened to Sul, probably it didn't happen in this car."

That was a relief. I hadn't dared ask him about the trunk. I'd wakened up with an ugly image in mind and couldn't quite shake it: Tim Sullivan wrapped in translucent plastic, his face slightly blurred, his eyes wide and utterly still.

The Celtic Grill is located a few blocks from the McGrath Highway. It is neither a clean nor a well-lighted place, despite the fact that the day bartender is a dead ringer for Ernest Hemingway, although I doubt the great man ever let his fingernails get that black. The freight yards are visible through the smoky plate glass, and railroad men are the primary customers. It's a whiskey-straight kind of place. They've got microwaved pizza, for those who don't know better, and draft beer that has the unmistakable tang of a moldy tap.

Larry Sheehan was right at home. He had two cigarettes going when I found him. One in the ashtray and the other clinging to his lower lip. After acknowledging my presence with a tight frown, he downed a quick beer and a shot, then ordered a follow up. I decided to risk a coffee. It came with a dose of Irish whiskey, like it or not.

Sheehan scowled and ground out one of the Luckies. "Nobody saw nothin'" he said, indicating the hunched bar patrons. "Typical. They could haul in the Statue of Liberty, cut it up for souvenirs, and nobody'd see nothin'."

The coffee burned like acid. I decided I liked the sensation and waved for another. Hemingway nodded with a distinct lack of enthusiasm, as if he wished me a short, unhappy life.

"You're checking out the neighborhood just in case," I said.

"Yeah, sure. I got four guys going door to door. Ain't no neighborhood here, though. Mostly warehouses and dives like this. Where nobody knows nothin'." Sheehan raised his voice for the last phrase. The shoulders at the bar hunched lower. "Fuckin' cretins. I tell 'em there's a cop's life at stake, they look at me like, so what?"

A long, slow-moving train rattled through the freight yard. The tracks screamed. Sheehan scowled. It was a great way to start the day.

"What about Calvino?" I asked. "Maybe Sully went looking for him."

Sheehan exhaled thoughtfully. "Yeah," he said. "Maybe. Only we got no witness to that."

"So you talked to Fat Lenny?"

"Sure, for what it was worth. Went down there to the Club Palermo where he and his cronies sit around drinking those little cups of wop creosote, or whatever it is. Let 'em check me for a wire, which it makes my skin crawl, allowing those creeps to lay a finger on me. And that fat fuck Calvino kept staring at me, and that pisses me off, too. I hate it when a slug like that stares at me. It ain't human, somehow."

"Let me guess," I said. "He's never heard of Tim Sullivan, or Leland Maddock."

"Nah, he was cuter than that. Explained how he'd read about Sully in the paper. Which I'm assuming somebody read it to him, 'cause I'm pretty sure the bastard is illiterate. Anyhow, like I figured, he expressed his shock and outrage that someone would try to take out a cop and lay the blame on him. Maddock he knows nothin' about. Never heard of General Gritz or *American Mercenary*. So he says."

"You mention Liam Delaney?"

"Not by name. I said an informed source in the police department had heard Sully had done something to offend a woman in Calvino's family. He got a kick out of that. Shook like a bowl of jello. He says, 'Detective Sheehan, I would be proud to have any of the bitches in my family get it on with an officer of the law. I always wanted a cop in the family.'"

After everything was over, after the last piece of the puzzle slipped into place, the one thing that was crystal clear was that I should have told Sheehan about going to see Kid Tony. Instead, I made a conscious decision to keep that information to myself. I liked the idea of knowing something Sheehan didn't. I thought it gave me an edge. The edge it gave me was, in the end, sharp enough to kill an innocent man.

Sheehan, to give him credit, sensed I was keeping something back, but he was just too emotionally exhausted to make me come clean. An ambulance siren doo-wopped down the highway. His eyes flicked away and he let it go.

We ended up sitting in the Celtic Grill for an hour or so, making psychobabble about the late Leland Maddock, soldier for hire and would-be Rambo. Sheehan liked to throw around the psychiatric jargon and I had no objection—it was easier than admitting we didn't know if Tim Sullivan was alive or dead.

"Guess what, I been over the Vets to see the shrink runs the outpatient program," he said, working on his third beer. "Mister Leland Maddock made a definite impression."

"You talked to his psychiatrist?"

"Sure I did. Tried to give me that crap about doctor-patient privilege. I said to the shrink, 'This is not a patient no longer, Doc. This is a corpse. What are you, an undertaker, you got to protect the body?' He didn't like that."

"No sense of humor," I said.

"None," Sheehan agreed. "Anyhow, the word on Maddock, he was a paranoid schiz with sociopathic tendencies. Like we hadn't already figured that, right? I say to the shrink, 'Doc, every day I get to see sociopaths in action. Most of 'em are running for office, or trying to sell me insurance. It's the real psychos that worry me. The ones who kill for a thrill. Or for money.'"

"He know anything about Maddock's ambition to be a soldier of fortune?"

Sheehan nodded. "More or less. The doc was aware Maddock wanted to get back into the service. Obsessive about it. Only there was no way. The marines booted him on a psychiatric discharge and they didn't want any more of what he was selling. The way the shrink put it, he said, 'Leland had a spooky personality. He made people uncomfortable.' I say 'Doc, what this boy wanted to do was make people *dead,* did he ever mention that?'"

"Did he?"

"If he did, the shrink won't admit it. They tend to get real nervous when their 'clients' do unsociable things like bomb cars and shoot at police officers. Puts 'em in a bad light. So the shrink would like to blame it all on drugs."

"Drugs?" I said, recalling Maddock's chock-full medicine cabinet.

"Yeah, in the sense he wasn't taking his medication. Psychotropics. Sounds like a hot vacation spot, huh? Come on down to the psychotropics, get your ashes hauled."

"You tell him about Maddock's collection of jars?"

"Yep. Wanted to zing him with that one, but he took it

in stride. Says a lot of wackos save their bodily wastes. For instance, Howard Hughes. Guy had a couple billion dollars, he felt compelled to save his caca. Pathetic, huh? The way the shrink explained, it's fear of losing part of the body. Regressive infantile behavior. Or it could be paranoid delusions about being poisoned, which fits our boy."

I got pretty sloshed keeping up with Sheehan. He seemed content, fogging the air with his cigarettes, getting a mild buzz from boilermakers that would have stood me on my head. He was starting in on war stories about his early days on Vice when my bladder compelled me to either leave or risk embarrassment.

"Yeah, sure, take off. The comforts of home, I can understand that," he said, indicating that he wanted another drink. "One thing I forgot, you might get a kick out of this. Maddock wanted his shrink to write him a recommendation for this job he'd applied for. Guess what job?"

"He wanted to get on the cops?"

Sheehan grimaced. "Give me a break, huh? Maddock wanted a job as groundskeeper on this big estate out in Pride's Crossing."

"Are you serious?"

"I kid you not, and he got the job, too," he said, upending his glass. "Mowing the lawn for General George Gritz. Makes you wonder, don't it?"

The telephone crouched like an enormous black bug. A living thing that pulsed. It took all of her courage to pick up the receiver and drop the coin into the slot.

The first time she dialed the operator cut her off almost immediately. "Sorry, ma'am we can't give out the room number. Hotel policy."

So she had to resort to subterfuge. Trembling, she dialed again.

"Operator? I just got a call from Miss Bangs, the movie director, and I'm returning the call. Can you put me through?"

"Hold on."

She held on, throttling the receiver with both hands. It was alive. It was breathing. It wanted to get inside her head.

"Hello? Who's this?"

She began to speak, using all of her Voices.

CHAPTER TWELVE

"YOU'RE MAKING THIS UP," MEGAN SAID.

"Cross my heart. Ernest Hemingway is not dead. He's tending bar at the Celtic Grill."

Megan squinted at me. "You have such a warped imagination," she said. "That bothers me."

"All novelists are liars," I sniffed. "It's a way of life. We lie to get at the truth."

Megan looked dubious. It was the look she gave a manuscript before skewering it with a sharp blue pencil. I carefully backed out of range.

"Two phone calls," she said. "The first was from Marilyn. No word on Sully's whereabouts. And they've had to scale down the search."

"What!"

"Orders from headquarters. Larry's still got his little squad on the case but it seems the commissioner decided a full-scale manhunt was, quote, unproductive."

Meaning too expensive. All part of the urban dilemma. The first thing that gets cut from the budget is loyalty. Followed closely by common decency.

The other shoe didn't drop until an hour or so later. I was taking my ease in the kitchen, sipping at a bottle of beer and watching Megan expertly trepan a head of lettuce for the dinner salad when I remembered the second phone call.

"You said I got two calls," I said. "The first was Marilyn. Who was the other?"

The knife chunked through the lettuce. "Her," Megan said dismissively.

"Her have a name?" Silly question. Had to be Lindy Bangs.

"Said it was life or death," Megan said. "I have my doubts."

And her nerve. I dialed through to Lindy's suite and let it ring for a while. Which, at the Ritz, sounds like a cash register ringing up money. I hung up and started pushing back into the kitchen to share my thoughts with Meg on the subject of undelivered messages, when the phone rang. It was Lindy.

"I was hiding in the bathroom," she whispered. "It *was* you calling, wasn't it?"

"Lindy," I said, "why were you hiding? What's wrong?"

"They're going to kill me," she said. "I just know it."

"What? Who's going to kill you?"

Her voice was weak and distant, that of a small child calling from the bottom of a well. "The crazy lady," she said. "Saint Teresa."

"What are you talking about?"

"I'm afraid," she whispered. "*Really* afraid."

"I'll call the police."

"No!" She caught her breath. "They're part of it."

"The cops? Part of what?"

She tried to tell me. It didn't make any sense at all.

In the kitchen Megan was quartering tomatoes. The juice on her fingers looked like fresh blood. I said, "Lindy's in trouble."

"So?"

"Real trouble," I said. "Are you coming?"

The Ritz-Carlton is about ten blocks away. Not worth getting the van out of the garage and fighting the lights. I pushed hard while Megan jogged along beside me. The sidewalks were wet and the fine spray thrown by the wheels made my hands slick. Naturally I'd forgotten my gloves. I knew Meg was dubious about the necessity of rushing over to check on Lindy Bangs. *Silly bitch*, she'd said under her breath, and then shrugged when I caught her eye.

The crazy lady. Also known as Saint Teresa, apparently. Sully had been threatened by a crazy-sounding woman. So had the film company. Now it was Lindy. A pattern was beginning to emerge, although as yet it didn't make any sense. If the crazy lady was as unbalanced as she sounded maybe it never would.

Unless "crazy" was part of the cover. Leland Maddock had been disturbed, no doubt, but a willingness to kill for money is not, in this society, a definition of insanity. If it were, a professional thug like Fat Lenny Calvino would be wearing a straitjacket instead of an expensive Italian suit. A murder-for-hire is rarely committed in response to the urgings of invisible voices—unless you consider greed an invisible voice.

I was thinking about rosary beads immersed in blood when we entered the hotel. Had that nasty little stunt been intended as a symbolic threat? If so, what did it mean? Maybe Sully had understood, and that knowledge had resulted in his disappearance.

"You okay?" I asked.

Megan nodded, keeping up with me with long, loping strides. "This better be for real," she warned me.

The Boston Ritz is a favorite of touring celebrities. Movie stars and visiting royalty opt for the understated elegance and unobtrusive, round-the-clock room service that is unheard of in a typical convention hotel. There is nothing flashy about the Ritz-Carlton lobby, no looming atriums or mirrored ceilings, just a small front desk, a concierge, and a couple of elevators. Money in the lowest key, as steady and unadorned as a Mozart concerto.

On my first visit I'd found Miss Bangs lounging in silk, stroking a pregnant, blue-eyed cat named George. Living the champagne life. Now the sparkle was off the high and the stunning redhead looked as if she'd been living in a closet. At first she wouldn't even open the door.

"I'm a mess," she said, showing one bloodshot eye through the crack. "I'm so ashamed."

"Lindy, take the chain off the hook, okay?"

"It's just, you know, I'm so scared."

"We can't help if you keep us out in the hallway," I said.

"Who's that with you?" she said, her voice clouding with suspicion. "Is she a cop?"

"This is Megan, my significant other. You've already been introduced."

After a little more prodding she took the chain off and let us into the suite, then immediately scurried into the bathroom and shut the door. Retreating into the inner sanctum now that the moat was down.

Megan hissed, "Significant other?"

"Dumb," I admitted. "What would you prefer? Lover, girlfriend, fiancée?"

"Anything but roommate, I guess," Meg said. "Only significant other sounds like something from outer space."

"How about, 'This is Megan, light of my life.'"

"Much better. What's she *doing* in there?" Meg said, nodding at the bathroom. "This is one weird lady."

The weird lady emerged after a few minutes, holding a face cloth to her nose. The silk kimono no longer looked sexy. Just wrinkled and slept in.

"My nose is bleeding," she explained.

"Keep your head back," I advised. "What happened to George?"

"Who?"

"George the pregnant cat."

"Had kittens," she said, sitting on the unmade bed. "They took her away."

A thread of blood trickled from her nose. Megan decided to play doctor. She took charge, instructing Lindy to put her head back on a pillow. The young filmmaker seemed to welcome the attention. I was astonished by what a few days—and nights—had done to her. The youthful vitality and exuberance seemed to have evaporated, leaving behind an aura of weariness and fear. The wasted look and the trickle of blood convinced me that Lindy Bangs had been powdering her nose with something a lot stronger than talcum.

"You said someone threatened to kill you," I said.

She tried shaking her head but Megan was holding her steady, blotting up the nosebleed with a face cloth. "Not exactly," she said. "I think they want to. That's the impression I got, you know?"

I was glad Meg had agreed to come along. Her presence seemed to have a calming effect. Or maybe whatever Lindy had ingested in the bathroom had started to kick in. Whatever the reason, she started to make sense. Relatively speaking.

"Clarence got the first few calls," she said, referring to Clarence Higgs, the production manager. "Never mentioned it to me at the time. Just another crazy trying to reach out and touch someone. Celebrity stalkers. You always get a few when you shoot a movie. Then poor Clarence gets this gruesome package in the mail. A Catholic thing, you know, a cross?"

"A crucifix?"

"Yeah, that. It's got this dried stuff all over, could be blood. Clarence shows it to me. I say, ick! Get away! Figured it was stage blood, maybe. Only Clarence, who happens to be a Catholic, he's taking it seriously. He's really spooked. Says this woman who keeps calling, she sounds demented. Dangerous. Tells me he's going to beef up security on the set."

"This woman have a name?" I asked.

Lindy shrugged. The bleeding had stopped but she kept her head back on the pillow, where her thick red hair fanned out, framing her face. Camille with freckles. "Teresa, I think. Clarence called her Saint Teresa because of the crucifix, and the way she goes on about Heaven and Hell and meting out divine punishment. Okay, I didn't really pay much attention. It was Clarence's problem. He handles the screwballs, part of his job. Then what happened, he went back to the New York office after we suspended the shoot and the woman starts calling me here at the hotel. The first time I just, you know, hung up, and the second time she says if I hang up on her again I'll die."

"She said she'd kill you?"

"Not exactly that. More like, you know, God would strike me dead. So I listened to her."

"Can you remember what she said?"

Lindy smiled. It was not a happy kind of smile. More a nervous twitch. "That's the trouble," she said. "I can't forget. I want to but I can't, you know? The first thing, she goes: 'Paulie can't get into Heaven. They won't let him in.' So I go to her, I say, 'What the hell are you talking about, lady?' and then she kind of makes these little screaming noises—I mean really scary, okay?—and she says, 'Paulie is dead, they killed him, they made him die.'"

"Did she say who Paulie was, or who killed him?"

"Yeah," Lindy said. "She said he was a cop and the cops killed him."

CHAPTER THIRTEEN

THE SMART THING WOULD HAVE BEEN TO pick up the phone and inform Detective Sheehan that the woman who had been threatening Sully over the phone was somehow connected to a deceased police officer, first name Paul. Let Sheehan take it from there. It was, after all, a police matter.

However, when it comes to police matters I rarely do the smart thing—witness the piece of lead in my spine—and instead tend to rely on my own worst judgment. They say that awareness of one's deficiencies is the first step on the road to recovery. They're wrong. Repeating past mistakes is the most human trait of all. Look at history. Look at me.

What I figured was that if the police commissioner had scaled down the manhunt there had to be a reason. Something even more crucial than exceeding the budget. And if the head cop was compromised, what chance did a mere detective like Sheehan have?

That was my reasoning. Or my excuse.

"Whoever she is, she's not just a little crazy," Lindy was saying. "She's a *lot* crazy, okay? Keeps mentioning the voices in her head. How they make her do this or that."

"And you think she's a local?"

Lindy nodded. "Distinct Boston-type accent. They could use her on *Cheers*," she added with a nervous giggle.

"This Teresa, did she mention how Paulie was related to her? Friend, husband, brother, son?"

Lindy was still giggling. Very quietly. "All of the above," she said. "Whoever Paulie really was, he's God Almighty as far as this lady is concerned, okay?"

Rosary beads. Crucifix. Blood. Saints and martyrs. A strong undertone of religion, to say the least. But the late Paul, last name unknown, was a cop, not a priest. And Teresa, last name unknown, had been disturbed by the fact that a cop movie was being shot locally. There was nothing religious about that, nor was religion a factor in the Casey book the movie was based on. It didn't make sense. Unless the religious angle was a cover, a diversion.

I kept thinking about Fat Lenny, and the rumors that Tim Sullivan had somehow offended the crime boss by dalliance with a female of the Calvino family. Maybe there *was* something to it.

"This crazy Teresa," I said. "She ever mention Fat Lenny Calvino?"

"Who?"

"Local choir boy," I said.

"You gotta understand," Lindy said, lifting her head from the pillow. "The woman is wacko. Heavy-duty nuts. What she says doesn't make sense. The TV set talks to her. Light bulbs talk to her."

Megan made it obvious that I should cease and desist

from interrogating the patient. Sisters united against the insensitive male. Couldn't I see that poor Lindy was overwrought? All that without saying a word. Is it any wonder I had proposed marriage?

The fact remained that Lindy was in tough shape. She was strung out on something more than fear of the phone calls and the anxiety of having her movie put on hold. Something had dilated her pupils and made her nose bleed. There wasn't much I could do about the drugs or the movie delay, but I did know a way to make the threatening phone calls stop.

All it required was an appeal to sisterhood.

"Meg," I said. "I think we should get Lindy out of here, agreed?"

Megan nodded, "Agreed."

"Now wait a minute," Lindy said, sitting up.

"Take our guest room for a few days," I suggested. "Saint Teresa can't call if she doesn't know where you are. Later you can book into another hotel under a different name. Or this hotel, for that matter. By then she'll be focused on someone else."

"I'll take a couple of sick days," Megan said, warming to the idea. "We'll do something silly like bake cookies, get your mind off this weirdness."

It didn't really take all that much persuasion. Lindy was alone and frightened and the idea of female company appealed to her. Having known Megan for less than an hour, she was ready to trust her, which is the normal reaction women have to Meg.

"I'll have to call Clarence," she said.

"Fine. Call from our place and give him our number. Ask him not to divulge it. That'll keep the crazies off your back. We're supposed to have clear, dry weather in a few days, so before you know it you'll be back out shooting, right?"

"Right," she said without much confidence. "I'll just get a few things together."

Boys' night out. Russ White suggested we meet at Faraday's, a little bar near Scollay Square. I can call it Scollay Square again now that the city in its wisdom has gone back to the original name, although every vestige of the notorious saloon row was demolished years ago in an orgy of urban removal. I like to think the ghost of the old place lingers there despite the sterile severity of the modern plaza that replaced it.

The barroom was at street level—no stairs to navigate—enabling me to gain entrance without making a production out of it. Chalk one up to Russ for suggesting the place. Street-level saloons are rare in Boston. It is part of the Puritan ethic to punish imbibers by making them climb at least a few creaky stairs in pursuit of a drink.

Russ waved from the bar as I wheeled into the cheerful, smoky interior. Because of the proximity of Government Center, Faraday's was popular with the political crowd—midlevel bureaucrats, not the heavy hitters from the State House. Lots of pinstripe suits, County Clare faces, and sturdy elbows. A perpetual chorus of 'Another please, and one for my good friend' echoed off the high ceilings. The lights were kept at a level sufficient to permit the reading of newspapers, an activity in which more than a few were engaged.

Russ had two drinks in hand by the time I worked my way through the crowd. He blazed a trail to a table in the rear, a spot of relative tranquillity.

"Took the liberty of securing you a Crested Ten," he said, handing over a glass of Jameson's finest Irish whiskey. "We're on the cuff," he added with a grin, meaning that his paper would pick up the tab.

"You look cheerful," I said.

"And why not?" the reporter said, sipping his drink. "Devlin is happy, ergo I am happy."

Hugh Devlin had raised circulation and advertising revenues for the McGary chain, which owned the *Standard,* by improving sports coverage and crime reporting. The word on the street was that to make it into the tabloid a story had to score or bleed. The personality conflict between Russ and Devlin stemmed from the fact that the publisher was young, rich, handsome, and the product of an exclusive business school, while Russ was none of the above. He just happened to be the best crime reporter north of Miami.

"And what makes Devlin happy?" I asked.

"Wading through money in his silk socks," Russ said. "That's high on the list. The other thing that turns Devlin on is cop stories. Brave cops, bad cops, smart cops, dumb cops, whatever. So when I told him I was about to get a break in the Sullivan case, he started wagging his tail and told me I could go top shelf on the expense account."

I grinned. "Hurray for the Crested Ten. This may not be much of a break, though, Russ. And you can't use it until we see where it goes."

"Trust me," Russ said.

"I hear that phrase, the back of my neck starts to itch."

"Get a haircut," Russ advised. "Right now I want to make sense out of this crazy mess." He began to tick items off on his fingers. "So far we have a canceled movie about a homicide detective, an attempt on the life of a real homicide cop, which results in a dead mercenary. Then the aforementioned homicide cop disappears. Plus we got a whole lot of rumors. Let's sort it all out, shall we?"

"Wait a sec," I said. "Back it up there. A canceled movie? Don't you mean delayed on account of rain?"

"What," Russ scoffed, "like a freakin' baseball game? The word is the Casey flick is all done. Finis. Various reasons, of which weather problems are the least. Dope-addict director, leading man who wants out, over budget, lack of network interest in the product, take your pick."

"Jesus," I said, "Christ."

"Hey," Russ said. "These things happen. If it makes you feel any better I also heard the film company is going to try and put together what they've got and sell it as a pilot to a cable network."

I looked at my glass. It was empty. "Hit me again," I sighed.

"Don't feel bad," Russ said as he signaled for another round. "Hey, these are just rumors we're discussing."

"I hate rumors," I said.

"Don't be silly. Life is a rumor. Try to nail it down and, poof!, all gone."

"Spare me the dime-store philosophy, Russ. You asked about a connection between the movie and the fact that Sully is missing. I don't think there is one—not a rational connection, anyhow."

"How about the magazine, *American Mercenary*. Were they in on it?"

I shrugged. "Beats me. I think that down deep General George Gritz is at least as wacky as the late and unlamented Leland Maddock. The difference is Gritz is very wealthy. He can live out his fantasy, channel his violent tendencies. It's no coincidence that Maddock was the type gets glorified in his magazine: a paranoid obsessed with virility, weapons, and killing. I'm sure Gritz knew that when he hired him. But was the general involved in the attempted murder? Doubtful. Why would he be? Not for the money, surely. And if he has an urge to kill someone he can fly down to Central America and play war games with one of the terrorist groups he helps sponsor. He doesn't need to put a hit on a cop, or arrange to have him disappeared."

"So the Gritz connection is an anomaly?"

I laughed. "I wouldn't have described him that way, but now you mention it, yes."

"Too bad," Russ said. "He's good copy."

"Forget Gritz," I said. "Let's concentrate on Saint Teresa."

"Who?" Russ said, perking up.

Without bringing Lindy Bangs into it, I told him what I knew about Teresa and Paulie. Paul a cop, now dead, and Teresa a probable schizophrenic currently obsessed with Paul's death, which she blamed on other cops, notably Tim Sullivan. For reasons as yet unknown.

"Somehow she's connected Sully with the Casey movie. Probably read your piece in the *Standard* alluding to Casey being based on Sully's career."

"Uh-huh," Russ said, letting the zinger pass. "So we check out any recently dead cops, first name Paul with wife/sister/mother name of Teresa. Is that the idea?"

"That's it. There is one little problem."

Russ raised his sandy eyebrows.

"Teresa may not be her real name," I said. "Maybe she just identifies with Saint Teresa."

"Beautiful," Russ said. "Well, I guess I should be grateful for one thing."

"What's that?"

"Could be worse," he said, gazing at the crowd around the bar. "The dead cop could be named Pat."

The first thing I noticed in the apartment was the smell of burning cannabis. The bright tinkle of female laughter drifted from the living room. My entrance set off a fresh round of giggles. No doubt due to my involuntary facial expression, what Megan calls my bulldog look.

"Uh-oh," Lindy said, "I think we're under arrest."

The redhead looked vastly improved by the change of venue. A thin cashmere sweater and tight slacks showed off her small-waisted, big-busted figure. It was obvious there was nothing but bare flesh under the cashmere. Her eyes, like Megan's, were smoky red.

"Oh, hi," Meg said. "We were just, um. . . ."

Meg knows I disapprove of her occasional use of marijuana. Not because of the drug itself, which I consider relatively harmless in moderation, but because of the peculiar way it affects her. After a few tokes she becomes withdrawn, distant, retreating into a private world. Leaving me on the outside. Knock, knock, can Megan come out and play? No answer.

"How'd it go with, um, Russ?" she asked, trying to act straight.

"Fine," I said. "He's going to run the names through his computer files, see what pops up."

"We've been having a great time," Lindy said.

"I can see that," I said, then changed my tone. "I mean good. Great. Glad to hear it."

I was trying to lighten up. Surely a little marijuana was no big deal, compared to what Lindy had been ingesting recently. I ought to be happy that the two of them were getting along so well, considering that not so very many hours before Meg had been referring to Lindy as "her" and "that bitch." Maybe *that's* what was bothering me. That Meg had discovered she had no cause for jealousy.

I'd rather hoped she did. Purely for reasons of ego enhancement.

"You want a hit?" Lindy said, oblivious to the slight strain her presence had caused.

"I'll pass."

"There's good news, Jack," Meg said. "Lindy's going back to work."

For some reason that produced another storm of giggles.

"I talked to Clarence," Lindy said, wiping her eyes. "We're on for next week. Five shooting days and then we wrap. Rain or shine."

I opened my mouth. "You're kidding," I said. "I just heard that . . . never mind."

Lindy gave me a cunning look. "You heard we'd been canceled, right?"

"Well," I said. "Yes."

"Rumor," Lindy said. "Malicious gossip. We're three-quarters of the way done. Nobody pulls the plug when they have that much in the can."

"And Burt Bardo?"

"Will honor his contract. That's straight from the lawyers. We had an Act of God clause in there and as near as anyone can determine inclement weather is an act of God. So Bardo stays. And it may be a moot point anyway, because I heard his big action flick is in turnaround."

"Really?" I said. "Where'd you hear that?"

"Rumor," Lindy said.

That set off the giggles again. What the hell, I thought, and joined in.

CHAPTER FOURTEEN

THAT WAS TUESDAY NIGHT. BY WEDNESDAY
evening I was on Fat Lenny Calvino's list of unfavorite
people. A shitbird, as the big man called anyone who
had the misfortune to irritate him. The way Fat Lenny
looked at it, the world was full of shitbirds. Cop shitbirds, reporter shitbirds, lawyer shitbirds, and at least
one writer shitbird. Me.

I was still blissfully ignorant of my avian status on
Wednesday morning. The day started off with a bang, so
to speak, when Lindy wandered into the kitchen wearing
a black tanktop and little else. The legend across her
breasts said: BETTER RED. In blazing red letters, of
course.

"Hi," she said.

Meg was out for her morning run, circling the Es-
planade.

"Hi," I said, making an effort not to inhale coffee
through my nose. "Sleep well?"

"Like a baby." She yawned and stretched to demonstrate. Thereby lifting the tank top to reveal a pair of translucent red bikini underpants.

Yow.

"Like some OJ?" I asked and busied myself with the juicer. Amazed at how the color red tended to resonate in my peripheral vision.

Down, boy, I thought. *It's just a tease.*

Easier thought than done. When I handed Lindy the glass of fresh juice she leaned down and kissed me. On the mouth, with just a tickle from her tongue.

"That's for being so sweet," she said. "For coming to my rescue."

"Huh?"

"For taking me in, silly."

"Oh," I said. "You're very welcome. It wasn't like we took you in off the street, Lindy. You were installed at the Ritz, remember?"

"Hush," she said, placing a finger on my lips. "I was having an itsy-bitsy nervous breakdown and you had the wisdom to get me out of there."

"And Meg," I said. "Her, too. I mean it was her idea, too."

"And Megan," Lindy agreed. "What a sweet kid. You two are getting hitched, huh?"

"Right," I said. "Christmas Eve."

"What?"

"We're getting married on Christmas Eve. In Nantucket. That's where her mother lives."

"The island?"

"Huh?"

"The island of Nantucket?"

"Right," I said, clearing my throat. "The only Nantucket, far as I know. Island or otherwise."

"That's where the whales live, right?"

"Uh, not exactly. Whalers used to live there. The

whales they hunted were halfway round the world, usually. Nowadays what you get in Nantucket is a lot of people with whales printed on their pants, and their socks, and their belt buckles. It's not quite the same."

Lindy sipped the juice and smiled secretly and watched me watching her. Getting a kick out of me getting a kick. I felt like a teenager. Any minute I was going to break out in pimples.

"You still mad about the script?" she asked. "You know, the changes?"

"I've learned to think of it this way," I said. "I wrote a book and you're making a movie. The movie isn't the book. There's no point of comparison, therefore no reason for me to bitch about it."

"It must be hard," she said. And giggled, batting her eyelashes. "I mean giving up your baby. Your book."

I shrugged. Pretty sure my ears were as red as her bikini underpants. "It's no big deal," I said. "I have to admit, for a while I was offended you thought my screenplay needed revision. See, I'd already revised it about six times."

Lindy smiled. "And I unrevised it."

"Yes."

"You're still offended," she said, putting her hands on her hips and cocking her pelvis. Like she had a pair of six-guns strapped to her hips. "Tell me you're not still offended."

Get a grip on yourself, Hawkins.

"I'm not," I said, gulping. "I'm not. Really. It's okay."

Why did I feel like she was making me beg forgiveness? And why did I like doing it?

"So," I said. "Shall I toast you an English muffin? Or would you prefer an egg?"

Lindy put her hands on the arms of my chair. Her feet

were spread wide. "You know what I really want?" she asked.

"Uh, what?"

The telephone rang before she could answer, or demonstrate. Saved by Ma Bell.

The old *Boston Standard* building used to be on Causeway Street, a few staggers from the Garden. It was a seedy, antiquated place with a big, smoky newsroom right out of *The Front Page,* and presses thundering in the basement. When the McGary syndicate entered the picture they razed the building, sold the vacant lot to developers, and moved the editorial offices into pristine new quarters on Congress Street. The new hi-tech printing plant is in Brighton, so you can no longer smell ink at the *Standard.* Or cigars or cigarettes. No smoking on the premises, thank you.

A few of the more rebellious sportswriters have taken to using snuff. They recently petitioned for a communal brass spitoon but were denied the privilege. Too bad. The sight of bleary-eyed men drooling into paper cups while staring at blank computer screens is disconcerting. Is this the New Journalism? Only publisher Hugh Devlin knows for sure, and being sensible he doesn't grant interviews. Not ever.

Russ White was waiting in his cubicle. He looked like a cat who had ingested a succulent canary and was resisting the temptation to spoil the sanctity of the moment by burping feathers.

"Give," I said.

"Patience," Russ said. "First I want you to appreciate all the trouble I went to. You got any idea how many cops in the Greater Boston area have the given name Paul? Huh? Or how hard it is to cross-reference for names of immediate family? Plus we had a problem with the alphabetical listings in the obit files because naturally they go by the last name. So what I did, I had to modify a program to cull by the first name, then run all the Pauls through again to turn up any with a Teresa listed under immediate family. Can you imagine what a pain that is? I was here most of the night trying to get the freaking program to run."

"Which it did or you wouldn't have called. Come on, Russ, what did the machine spit out? Who have we got?"

"Okay," he said. "We have one Paul Cotillo. Held the rank of sergeant in the Metro cops. Until he and his brother and about ten of their buddies were indicted in the Coke Box Bust. Remember that one?"

Coke Box Bust. That was tabloid for a scam wherein a group of uniformed cronies had swiped large quantities of drugs seized in busts and supposedly held for evidence. They replaced the cocaine with powdered sugar and put the real stuff back on the streets. A number of Metro cops got rich on the scheme, and none of them went to jail until they made the mistake of wholesaling some of the stuff to a DEA sting operation. The drop-off was a post office box on Washington Street. Hence the catchy headline.

"The prospect of going to prison made Mr. Cotillo despondent," Russ said. "He shot himself, leaving his wife Teresa."

So far it made sense, in a perverse kind of way. Unless it was just a coincidence. The woman who was making the threats had implied that her husband was betrayed by his fellow officers. I said, "Can I assume that Paul Cotillo was left out in the cold by his cop buddies?"

"You can. As you may recall there was a rather undignified scramble of dirty cops, all seeking to testify against their pals in exchange for immunity. Cotillo kept his mouth shut and it cost him. He was sentenced to fifteen years. Would have had to do ten the hard way."

"What do you have on his wife?"

Russ grinned. Burping metaphorical canary feathers. "I have two things," he said. "First she has a history of mental disturbance. The second is that her maiden name is, drum roll, please, Calvino. Teresa Calvino."

"I don't believe it."

"Hey," Russ said, leaning back in his chair. "The computer never lies."

"What's her connection to Fat Lenny?" I said, feeling out of breath for the second time that morning. "Daughter?"

Russ shook his head, amused by my reaction. "That would be too neat," he said. "I'm having trouble nailing down who she's related to, exactly, but for sure she's not part of Fat Lenny's immediate family. Daughter, wife, et cetera. There are a lot of Calvinos in the area, and they're not necessarily related to each other or to the Calvino crime family. Where exactly the widow Teresa fits in I can't say. Not yet."

"You have an address?"

"Of course I have an address," he said. "Tell you what. You do the driving and I'll do the talking."

"That's the second best offer I've had today," I said.

"Yeah? What was the first?"

I thought about Lindy Bangs in her red bikini panties and kept my mouth shut.

CHAPTER FIFTEEN

A PRODUCE TRUCK HAD CRASHED ON THE exit slope out of the Callahan Tunnel, locking us into a line of stalled and idling vehicles. This is how the world will end, not with a bang but a traffic jam. Nuclear gridlock. Pieces of fruit and vegetable rolled down from the scene of the accident, bumping into the tiled gutters. Russ got out of the van and returned with a big red apple.

"A Delicious," he said, dusting it off.

"You're going to eat that?"

He grinned and bit into the apple. "I'm a reporter," he said. "I take what I can get."

An hour or so later we were rolling through the rutted streets of East Boston, the airport ghetto cut adrift from the heart of the city. Dirty and gray and poor as it is, the neighborhood has, in my humble opinion, one huge advantage. Not even the most rapacious developer would dare attempt gentrification under the roaring shadows of the 747's that jelly the smog every minute or so. The only thing that gets refined in East Boston is oil.

"It's around here somewhere," Russ said, peering down side streets. "Maybe we should stop and ask directions."

"I prefer to keep my hubcaps, thanks."

Russ chuckled. "They take the whole wheel now," he said. "Nobody wants just the hubcap."

Eventually we located the address. One of a row of mauve ranch houses. I pulled up to the garage door and found myself eye to eye with a bald eagle. Styrofoam rampant on plywood.

"You sure this is the place, Russ?"

"According to the printout, Metropolitan Police Sergeant Paul Cotillo resided at this address until he shot himself."

"No curtains on the windows, Russ. No drapes. Looks empty."

I stayed behind the wheel. Russ got out of the van and went to the front door. He looked back at me, shrugged, and pushed the buzzer. He must have liked pushing the buzzer because he kept doing it. After a while he gave up and walked around to the back of the house, out of sight.

Five minutes later he returned, climbed into the van, and sighed. "Nobody home," he said. "No grieving widow, no furniture, no nothing."

"Like I said, empty. Maybe it's not the right house."

"Not quite empty," he said. "There's an outline of a body chalked on the floor of one of the back rooms. And a big brown spatter of stains on the wall behind it."

I thought about that for a moment. The Styrofoam eagle over the garage door had a crazy kind of look in its eye. "When was it Cotillo shot himself?"

"Six months ago," Russ said.

"Plenty of time to clean up his mess. What kind of wife would move out of the house and leave the chalk on the floor and the blood on the wall?"

Russ gave me a look. "The kind who doesn't want to forget?" he suggested.

At Russ's insistence we stopped at the Nite Flite Café, a converted Quonset hut within sight of the Logan air-cargo terminals. There was a portable sign in the lot that said LIVE STRIPPERS.

Russ saw it and chuckled. "Consider the alternative," he said.

"If you're desperate for a beer we can stop at 7-Eleven," I suggested.

"Come on," he said. "I want to check the place out."

"Why?"

"Because the manager is Pete Cotillo. Paul's younger brother. Also one of the many accomplices in the evidence room rip-off. You want to know how a convicted felon out on appeal gets a permit from the Liquor Commission to manage a bar?"

"He has friends in low places?"

"Something like that."

I followed Russ into the café, braced myself for the shifting glances a wheelchair usually elicits, and found that all eyes were on the stage. The stripper just concluding her performance was young, pretty, and very much alive. She was also totally nude, with a triangle of pubic hair that was dyed flame orange to match the wig on her head.

"The things I do for a story," Russ said.

"You love it."

The bar area was crowded. Most of the seats around the small stage were taken, all by males. Not bad for mid-afternoon in East Boston. A fair number of customers wore air-cargo coveralls. Winding down after a long shift, or maybe getting ready to punch in. Waitresses cruised the painted concrete floor, dressed in abbreviated hostess outfits. One of them veered our way. I assumed it was my encroaching middle age that made her look about twelve years old to me.

"What'll it be?"

"Couple of beers, I guess," Russ said. "Pete around?"

"Who?"

"Pete Cotillo. The manager."

The waitress glanced at the bar, where a brawny, baldheaded individual was pouring glasses of draft beer.

"Who's asking?" the girl said, trying to sound tough, which is hard to do with a mouth full of neon pink bubblegum.

"Friends of Teresa," he said. "Just mention her name."

The girl tottered away, not really at ease on stiletto heels.

"Cute," Russ said.

"Yeah, cute," I said, "like chicken pox is cute."

The waitress put her tray on the bar and spoke to the bruiser who was pouring beers. I saw his face go blank with fear. It lasted only a moment, until the waitress pointed us out. Then blank fear was immediately replaced by an expression of wary relief. He finished topping off a tray of glasses and then brought two beers over to our table.

"Girl said you wanted to see me," he said. Close up he was even bigger than he'd appeared while looming behind the bar. Under six feet but with a stevedore's arms and chest and the ruined knuckles of a street fighter. In Metro cop blues he must have been truly intimidating.

"State your business." he said.

Russ introduced us. He failed to mention his occupation. An oversight, no doubt. Pete Cotillo glanced at me. Glared might be more accurate. "You look familiar," he said. "I know you?"

I said, "I've got one of those generic faces."

"Huh?"

"I just look familiar," I said. "Why we're here, we're looking for your brother's wife, Teresa."

He rubbed a big hand over his bald head, which had the hard, oily sheen of an artillery shell. "Believe me, Teresa ain't here. You don't know the lady if you think she'd be in a place like this. Heaven forbid."

Russ said, "Mr. Cotillo, we—"

"Pete," he said. "Anybody calls me mister I figure they're bill collectors. I assume you ain't bill collectors?"

I said, "We think Teresa may have threatened a friend of ours. Over the phone."

"Yeah? What kind of friend?"

"A cop," I said.

The big man lowered himself into a chair.

"A cop?" he said. "Anybody I know?"

Another girl had taken the stage—or possibly the same girl with a new wig. Evidently minimal stripping was involved, since she started out with only pasties and a G-string.

I told Cotillo Sully's name and rank. He nodded slowly. "Yeah, I think I heard of him. Homicide Unit, right? Hey, wait a minute, he's the guy that turned up missing, right?"

I nodded.

Cotillo grimaced. "That freakin' broad," he said. "I tell 'em to lock her up and throw away the key, but nobody listens. Paulie, the poor bastard, he done that years ago, he'd be alive today. I tell him, a hundred times I musta gone, 'Paulie, for Chrissake commit her, okay? You don't have to divorce her, you don't want, but the woman needs help, she's eating up your life.' Which I didn't know the half of it at the time. All that crazy religious crap."

The girl on stage was squatting and spreading her legs, moving vaguely to a synthesized rock tune. She looked surprisingly cheerful, considering.

"So you never actually met her, Teresa?" Cotillo asked. "I got that right?"

"We've never met her," I said. "And we don't know for sure she's the one making the threats. Or if she has anything to do with Sullivan's disappearance. The woman we're trying to locate sounds crazy over the phone. Possibly schizophrenic. She hears voices, apparently. She talks about someone called Paulie, and how he was betrayed by the police. Sound like that could be your sister-in-law?"

He started nodding before I was finished. "Gotta be her," he said. "Freakin' woman was always nuts, my opinion, but she really went around the bend after Paulie died. I had a bad feelin' about her right from the start. Ten, twelve years ago when Paulie brings her home to meet the family. Thanksgiving dinner, right? I mean my first reaction, this is one beautiful girl. Black hair, big dark eyes. Like Sophia Loren only she didn't have the big tits. Tits or no tits, she was a knockout, *Capito*? Until she opens her mouth. It's like she'd start a sentence and by the time she finished, it was about something else entirely. Like she had the words inside out. Real spooky."

"Do you think she's capable of violence?"

Cotillo passed a meaty hand over his chin and thought about it. "I ain't no shrink," he said. "All I know, she's a crazy broad. Insane type of crazy. Paulie had to put her in the hospital a couple of times, it got so bad. Hearing voices, like you said. Sometimes it was God, sometimes it was Satan or some angel she made up. The funny thing is—only it ain't funny at all—it was always Teresa who was threatening to kill herself. And then it was Paulie who done it for real."

"Because he was facing time in prison?"

The big fists clenched. I got ready to duck, but when he finally answered, Pete Cotillo sounded puzzled, not angry. "Lemme tell you guys something. He was my own brother, but I got no idea why he done it. Just like I got no idea how come he stuck by Teresa all those years."

"Maybe he loved her," I said.

He gave me an odd look, like he thought I was jiving him. When he realized I was straight he sighed and said, "Yeah, I guess he did. The poor dumb bastard. You know he had an insurance policy, was supposed to help her if he died? Which of course she blew, handing cash out in the streets, sending it to charities. Like she had to get rid of it, it was dirty money."

"Maybe she thought of it that way."

He shrugged. "I give up trying to figure Teresa. All I know is, don't believe what you heard in the papers about Paulie. He weren't no bad cop. Not really. I wanted in on the deal because it was there, okay? I like money. For Paulie it was different. He didn't do it for himself. He wanted to put Teresa into this expensive clinic. The guy never stopped believing they could make her better, if only he had enough money."

"And that's why he got involved with the drug rip-off?"

"As God is my witness," Cotillo said. "He done it for Teresa."

CHAPTER SIXTEEN

WE CUT THROUGH EAST BOSTON AND GOT ON the ramp to the bridge, avoiding the tunnel. The traffic was just as bad but at least we were over the harbor instead of under it. Russ fidgeted in his seat and said, "Kind of gets you all choked up, huh? The devoted husband sacrificing himself for his schizo wife?"

"You don't believe it?"

"I was born a skeptic." Russ said dryly. "Hence my career in journalism."

Novelists tend to be skeptics also, but for me Pete Cotillo's story rang true. Over beers followed by shots of rye he had described the gradual deterioration of Teresa's psyche—and his brother's life.

In the early years Paul had been confident that his beautiful wife could be cured of her strange, frightening lapses into schizophrenia. Various therapists had tried various therapies. Analysis, regression, aversion, medication—whatever method was in vogue. Sometimes Teresa seemed to respond favorably and her illness went into remission for weeks or months. Inevitably, however, her demons returned. Sometimes she heard voices, or suffered from complex delusions involving vast conspiracies. She became manic, babbling wildly, talking to the air or the walls. But for her husband the worst periods were Teresa's "quiet" interludes, when she retreated into an unapproachable inner world. He could not reach her in that place. It was as if she existed behind a thick wall of glass. "Asleep with her eyes open" was how Pete Cotillo described it, or "dancing without a partner." Hardly clinical descriptions, but I got the picture.

"What happened," Pete had said, fingering his empty shot glass, "over the years Terry got crazier and crazier and Paul got sadder and sadder. Then he heard about the scam we were runnin' out of Evidence and told me he wanted in. And like a damn fool I let him do it. All the poor bastard did was carry a few payoff bags. Supposed to make a deposit over to this bank in Chelsea where we'd set up this joint account, right? No big deal. Only the bank is closed that day and Paulie leaves the dough in the trunk of his cruiser and the next day the DEA sting hits and they take Paulie with a hundred grand in marked bills. I tell him—I go, 'Paulie, for Chrissake tell the bastards whatever they need to hear. I'm your own brother and I'm beggin' you, go ahead and rat me out.' Only he won't do it. Never says a word. So when the indictments come down from the grand jury he gets hit the hardest. They put him on the stand, in my opinion a major mistake, and the DA makes him look like some kind of monster. Like he was the brains behind this horrible cop conspiracy. What a joke. And Paulie, he doesn't fight it. Tells me he doesn't care what happens to him. That strong and silent act of his, okay? Which I sort of believed, until finally he locks himself in the den and lights off his service revolver."

"Where was Teresa when he did it?"

The big man sighed. "She was in church. By then she'd been on this weird religious kick for a couple years. Normal people, they go to church on Sunday, right? But Terry, when she gets on a kick she always goes to extremes. Attends every mass. Lights every candle in every church for miles around, practically. Decides the voices she's been hearing all her life are really Jesus Christ, or Mary, or the devil—depending on her mood. And you got to feel sorry for the priests she pesters with all her visions and voices."

I said, "Here in East Boston?"

"Sure, until they got wise to her act. Then I think she started going back to her old neighborhood."

"Old neighborhood?"

Cotillo gave me a funny look. "The North End," he said. "That's where Terry come from. Wop City."

"She was attending churches in the North End?"

Cotillo shook his head and glanced at my wheels, no doubt equating dumb questions with disability. "That's what I said. Only I don't know if 'attending church' really covers it. Probably Terry was bugging the shit out of any priest would listen to her raving on about Christ and the devil and whatever invisible friends she's made lately."

When we took our leave of the Nite Flite Café a girl with neon green hair was straddling a toy airplane, fluttering her made-up eyes with mock urgency. Pete Cotillo had stared at me as we left, his eyes as empty as his shot glass.

I dropped Russ White off near Scollay Square.

"Maybe you better call Detective Sheehan," I suggested. "Bring him up to speed on this."

"My pleasure," he said with a wicked grin.

I waited until he was out of sight, then reversed direction and headed into the North End. Playing a hunch. Taking a risk I didn't care to share with a career skeptic.

The Club Palermo doesn't look like much from the outside. Come to think, it doesn't look like much from the inside, either. A fifties storefront with the glass painted black, a faded red door, and a small brass buzzer. The creature who answered the buzzer had just stepped out of a time machine. Direct from the Mesozoic, when giant reptiles ruled the earth. He had big shoulders, small eyes, and a tiny brain in his tail.

"Yeah?" he said, gazing down at me.

"You're already well over six feet tall," I said. "How come you wear elevator heels?"

"Huh?" he said.

"I'm here to see Mr. Calvino," I said, edging closer.

"Uh-uh," he said. "He don't see nobody."

"Pretty please?"

"Uh, go on. Get outa here. Dis ain't no public place."

I sighed. "Okay, the fun's over. Tell Fat Lenny I know he tried to have a cop killed."

"Mister, you're crazy."

"Just tell him."

Stegosaurus strode off, furrowing his brow as he attempted to retain the information. Overburdened with sensory input, he neglected to lock the club door. Being an impolite type, I entered uninvited. My first impression was olfactory: the place had a funk of sweet cigars, stale coffee, and hair tonic. There was thin carpeting on the floors, cheap paneling on the walls, and ceiling tiles the color of dirty snow. The Calvino brothers hadn't invested their ill-gotten gains in the Club Palermo, that much was obvious.

I turned down a narrow corridor and followed the faded foot track in the carpet. The cigar smell became sweeter, stronger. An undertone of guttural muttering became audible. I found myself in a small, dimly lit dining room. The smoke and the muttering originated from the far corner, where a rotund gentleman with a strangely blank face was deep in conversation with a familiar gray-haired gnome.

Fat Lenny's mugshots had appeared in the newspapers, naturally, but I'd never seen him in person. Consequently the odd, unchanging blankness of his expression came as a surprise. It was as if all evidence of emotion and personality had somehow been drained from an otherwise human face. Anthracite eyes picked me out as I entered the room, but that was his only reaction.

His gray-haired companion lacked Fat Lenny's placidity. Seeing me he did a double take, starting to bolt from his seat, then grinned and dropped back into his seat.

"Hello, Liam," I said.

I almost had time to wonder why Liam Delaney, of the police commissioner's office, was swapping cheap cigars with the prime target of a RICO investigation. Then the dinosaur picked up my wheelchair with me in it and I had to concentrate on more important things. Like the effect of gravity on falling objects.

CHAPTER SEVENTEEN

"LATER, MR. CALVINO," LIAM SAID, IGNOR-ing me.

The fat crime boss did not react as Delaney scurried from the club. Calvino merely gazed placidly at the spot in the air where I had been levitated by his henchman. A pudgy finger pointed to the floor. Stegosaurus sighed and put me down.

"Okay," Calvino said. "Talk."

It took me a few moments to get my breath back. Fat Lenny waited, a model of patience. It was hard to keep a fix on his entourage, but there seemed to be at least three other urban dinosaurs guarding the nest. Dark suits, pointy shoes, no necks. You didn't have to be psy-chic to pick up on the aura of small-minded malice they radiated. I got the impression that at a sign from the big man I would be instantly dispatched to the basement. Dropped right through the floor without benefit of ele-vator.

"It's about your crazy niece Teresa," I said uneasily.

"She tried to have a cop killed. Lieutenant Detective Timothy Sullivan. And now she may be responsible for his disappearance."

"My crazy niece?" he responded. "I have no crazy niece. I have five, six nieces, all normal."

I waited, expecting him to tap his pudgy fingers, or sigh, or roll his eyes, or make some small gesture that would indicate displeasure, or anxiety, or anger. Nothing. The man had the inner stillness of an empty concrete bunker.

"Teresa Calvino, or anyhow that was her maiden name," I said. "History of mental problems. Pretty, dark-haired girl from this neighborhood who married a Metro cop named Paul Cotillo. I think Terry's related to you somehow—maybe a niece, maybe a cousin—but the point is she tried to have a cop murdered and now the same cop is missing. And from what I can figure nobody has come forward with information because the word on the street is that Teresa has mob connections."

Fat Lenny pursed his lips. This is it, I thought. He's going to frown, or maybe smile. What he did was burp quietly and pat his mouth with a paper tissue.

"Think what they like," he said. "Ain't got no niece Teresa. So who's this cop got missing?"

"Tim Sullivan. Heads up the Homicide Unit. You want to know more about him, try asking the Weasel."

"Who?"

"Liam Delaney. The police commissioner's official brownnose."

Calvino was silent for a few moments. He rested his hands on his belly and shifted his bulk slightly. Setting up another intestinal discharge, perhaps. Maybe flatulence was his method of expression.

"Don't know no Delaney," he said.

"He was sitting right there when I got here," I said,

"small as life. Little skinny guy with gray hair and a bloodshot face. Eyes close together, hence his nickname."

"No," Calvino said.

"Kind of a droopy nose, no chin," I added.

"You make a mistake. No Delaney here," he said.

"Okay," I said. "Have it your way. No Liam Delaney. I must have been hallucinating. So forget I asked and just tell me, please, where I can find Teresa Cotillo, née Calvino."

Fat Lenny began to speak in Italian. The transition was unsettling, as if someone had slipped a different language tape into an overstuffed talking doll. He was not, I soon realized, speaking to me, but to one of his associates. The conversation went on for a while. My nine-word, menu-oriented command of the language was no help. I was pretty sure they weren't ordering out for pizza.

"Why?" Fat Lenny said eventually.

I stared, not certain he was addressing me.

"Why should I tell you about this crazy woman?" he said.

I shrugged. "Because a man's life is at stake? Because you're under indictment and you don't need any more trouble? Because it's polite to respond to a question? I don't know, Mr. Calvino. All I can do is ask and see what happens."

"Tell me more about what this woman has done."

So I told him as much as I knew, omitting the names of any individuals who might be the focus of unwanted attention from Fat Lenny or his pals. For instance Russ White, who had described him in print as "a humorless geek in a two-piece suit," and Larry Sheehan, who'd recently threatened to arrest him.

"Apparently Mrs. Cotillo is not in her right mind," I

said. "For some reason she has decided to blame her husband's suicide on Lieutenant Sullivan. First she harassed him over the phone, then she arranged to have a bomb planted in Sully's car. When the bomb failed to kill him she sent a weirdo named Leland Maddock into the hospital to finish the job, where he was shot and killed by the cops. A few days later Detective Sullivan disappeared."

Fat Lenny stared at me. Sidney Greenstreet with a fresh lobotomy. "Why should I know this woman? We got no crazy people in my family. No crazy Teresa."

I nodded. "It's like this. Teresa is an Italian girl from an Italian neighborhood."

"So?"

"Let me finish. She's not just any Italian girl from any Italian neighborhood. She has a last name in common with the family that has dominated the city crime scene for thirty years. Maybe she's somehow related, maybe not. But for sure when a neighborhood girl like Teresa decides she wants to hire an assassin, she'd come to you first."

"You the crazy one."

"Let me finish. She'd come to you and you'd turn her down because (A) she's obviously mentally disturbed and (B) she wants to kill a cop and you don't kill cops if you can help it." I paused and forced myself to smile. "How'm I doing?"

"I don't never kill cops," Fat Lenny said. "I don't never kill nobody."

And Ted Williams never hit a home run, I thought. "Okay," I said, "you weren't in the mood so Teresa hired an outsider. After Maddock was killed she may have hired someone else to abduct Lieutenant Sullivan. Or worse. I'm convinced Teresa is behind whatever happened to Sully, but you'll get the blame somehow. Just having the same last name will make it look bad."

Fat Lenny stared at me. Stared through me is more like it. He raised the crumpled tissue to his lips, appeared to kiss it.

"Wait here," he said.

He rose slowly, gliding from the room. Think of an olive-skinned dirigible venting quiet puffs of gas.

I waited. A hard, concussive sound interrupted my thumb-twiddling. I turned in my chair and noticed, for the first time, a pool table in the far end of the dimly lit dining room. Calvino's men were playing a game of who's behind the eight ball. They used cue sticks the way General Gritz used conspiracy theories. For the pleasure of intimidation. Slamming the balls around the table like jungle cats dicing with fresh skull bones, the boys were having fun.

I smiled and waved. They ignored me. When I turned Fat Lenny was back in his seat.

"Love to see what they'd do to a badminton game," I said.

His eyelids twitched. "Remember this, please, and tell your friends in the cops. This insane person Teresa is not in my family. *Capito*? I know only this about her: she claims to have visions of the Virgin Mary. Some people, neighborhood people, think that makes her a holy person. Like a saint or something. Stupid to think like that, right?"

"Maybe," I said.

"No maybe," Calvino said. "Is stupid. Like the priest who comes to ask me what should he do about this crazy woman who has been coming into his church. 'What should *I* do, Father?' I say. 'It is your church, do as you like. Have the woman arrested, have her put away.

Whatever you like.' So what does this stupid shitbird of a priest do? He does nothing."

"Priest?" I asked. "What priest?"

Calvino coughed into the tissue, crushed it, and dropped it to the floor. "Fabrizzi. A shitbird Neapolitan. You want to know more about this crazy woman, go ask him."

After the smoky gloom of the Club Palermo it was almost a surprise to see a clear, starlit sky over the North End. I made two phone calls from a booth on the street corner. The first was to the commissioner's office. I couldn't get through to anyone of consequence. An underling informed me that Liam Delaney had left early in the afternoon to attend an important meeting.

"I know he was at a meeting," I said. "He was meeting with a Mafia boss."

"Oh dear," the underling said, "another crank call."

I thought of a really good response shortly after he hung up. The next someone I tried to reach out and touch was Father Fabrizzi, pastor of St. Anthony's and patron of failed prizefighters. His housekeeper said that the priest was presiding over a funeral.

"Anyone I know?" I asked.

She ignored that. "The father is very busy. Funeral now, later a wedding, then he has the confirmation study group."

I left my name and number and got the distinct impression Father Fabrizzi was not likely to return my call.

"Very busy," the housekeeper said. "Very busy."

So it seemed.

The demon reached for her candle, drawn by the flame. She hissed and jerked back out of range.

"*Water,*" *he gasped, the word cracking in his throat.* "*Water.*"

Teresa crouched a few feet away. He could not move. He was in her power, and growing more feeble as each hour passed. Soon he would die, and pass back into Hell, whence he had come.

"*Back into the fire,*" *she taunted him.* "*And when you get there, take a message to my Paulie. Tell him you're sorry. You'll be sorry forever and ever, death without end. Amen.*"

He groaned, begged for water, and passed out.

Teresa hummed a song, a ditty from her childhood: ashes ashes, all fall down. She stared at the flickering candle until the flame guttered out. Then the darkness filled her, and she could feel the presence of her angels.

"*Cast him down,*" *she said in her sing-song voice.* "*He swore on the Bible and sent Paulie to Hell. Now you must cast him down. You must!*"

She crouched in a blaze of angel wings, making shapes with her hands, waiting.

CHAPTER EIGHTEEN

"SO A PRIEST LIED TO YOU," FITZY SAID. "SO what else is new?"

We were having breakfast in a Kenmore Square deli that served bagels the way Fitzy liked them, that is to say grilled until crispy and saturated with butter. The Irish version. Show Fitzy a plate of lox and he'd assume it was bait for a bigger fish.

"But why?" I asked. "He seemed so sincere."

"Why?" Fitzy said, licking his fingers. "You want to know why a priest lies to you? He lies because it's his nature. Because it's part of the job."

I shook my head and grinned. "Never got over parochial school, did you?"

"The bastards beat me with steel-edged rulers," he said, glancing at his knuckles as if expecting to see scars. "I dunno, Jack. Probably this priest is just scared of Fat Lenny. Which is a normal enough reaction. Guy has all the charm of an overweight gila monster."

Under a sparkling, late-September sky the city looked

crisp and dry. A good thing, considering that Lindy Bangs and her crew were setting up an expensive crowd scene right outside of Fenway Park. I was headed that way, hence our choice of a restaurant rendezvous.

"It was more than just fear," I said. "More than the usual deference parish priests have for influential criminals. That's what I thought at the time, but now I'm sure Father Fabrizzi was hiding something."

"You specifically asked him about this Teresa person?"

I tried the coffee. It tasted of chicory, which is fine if you happen to like the bitterness of chicory. I'm one of those old-fashioned fussbudgets who prefer coffee that tastes of coffee.

"I didn't have her name at the time," I said. "I told the father about Sully, though, and the crazy woman who had been threatening him over the phone. He'd have to be a fool not to put two and two together. He didn't strike me as a fool."

Fitzy winked. "I guess we're not that far apart, Jack, if you think priests are either fools or liars."

I sighed. "Fitz, I have nothing against the church and I like to think it has nothing against me. So let's not confuse the issue."

"*I'm* not confused."

"Yeah? Well, I am. Schizophrenia confuses me. Psychopathic soldiers of fortune confuse me. Attempted murder confuses me. Lawyers confuse me. Especially lawyers."

"What can I say?" Fitz asked happily. "You're a very confused individual. The way I see it, the thing is very clear. A nut decides she wants to kill a cop. She hired another nut to do the dirty deed. That didn't work. Now it looks like she hired someone else. Because I gotta tell you, Jack, Sully's been missing this long, chances are he's dead."

"Nobody knows that."

He shrugged. "Hey, I know you don't want to hear it."

"He's not dead until they find a body, okay?"

"Sure. Relax. So you really think this priest has a line on Teresa?"

I nodded. "I *know* he does. That's what Fat Lenny was telling me."

Fitzy was obviously skeptical. "My advice, make a donation to the poor box. Or maybe light a few candles. Play his game. Hey, you might even try going to mass."

"You're a big help," I said. "I'll handle the priest. What have you got on Liam Delaney?"

My friend Finian X. Fitzgerald has an eclectic law practice, to say the least. He and Lois set up housekeeping in the South End long before the place became trendy, and as the first lawyer on the block Fitzy agreed to be the mouthpiece for a number of community organizations. Leftist, nonprofit-type outfits that he calls his "pinko pals." He also does estate work for wealthy Back Bay clients, most of them decidedly eccentric. Back Bay pays the rent. Fitzy will also handle a lawsuit if it means he gets to perform in open court. Sometimes he represents petty criminals if (A) they have the money and (B) he's convinced they got a raw deal. "Raw deal" in Fitzy's world is defined as being innocent or, sometimes, being so unlucky as to get caught. It all depends on his mood and the balance, or lack of it, in his checking account.

The point is, Fitzy's range of work brings him into contact with every level of the state justice system. From crooked bondsmen to clean-as-the-driven-snow judges, from political hacks to charismatic statesmen. Everybody knows Finian Fitzgerald. Even a low-life like Liam Delaney. Hell, especially a low-life like Delaney.

"Ah, the Weasel," Fitz said. "What a guy."

"You talked to him?"

"Not exactly. We communed through intermediaries. His machine talked to my machine. Which means the Weasel is spooked. And you're the guy who spooked him, Jack, so felicitations are in order."

"He's on the take. Calvino is paying him off," I suggested.

"Hold on now. One thing at a time. Naturally Liam is on the take. He takes whatever he can get. But not, so far as I can discern, from the Calvino organization. What he wants from Fat Lenny is what they call a mute endorsement."

"A what?"

"Patience," Fitzy said, clearly amused. "The great Fitzgerald will explain. Through sources too numerous and craven to mention I have learned that the Weasel is not content with his sinecure as PR consultant to the commissioner. It pays a few pennies under forty large, plus expenses, but Liam is at a stage in life where, in order to feel whole and well and happy, he needs to have in his possession large sums of cash money. More than the petty graft that goes with his present job. So he wants to move up in the world."

"He thinks he can get the commissioner's job?" I said, astounded.

Fitz laughed. "Don't be silly. Not a chance. That takes an appointment from the mayor, and the mayor, no surprise, is of the opinion that Liam isn't fit to scour urinals at South Station. An opinion shared by many. Aware of this, Liam has decided to take his case to the electorate. What he's going to do, Jack, is run for city council.

142

Where his inability to swab out pissers will not be held against him."

"I don't believe it," I said. "The Weasel couldn't get elected dogcatcher."

"True enough," Fitzy agreed. "Only he isn't running for dogcatcher. He's running for city council. That's where before each meeting they play 'Send in the Clowns.'"

"Hasn't got a chance."

Fitzy shrugged. "Maybe, maybe not. Remember this is the same elective body that had Dapper "Pinhead" O'Neil as an honored member. And Louise Day Hicks. And many other splendid examples of democracy in action."

"I still don't get it," I said. "What was he doing brownnosing Calvino?"

Fitzy grinned. "You got it," he said. "That's exactly what he was doing. Trying to get Fat Lenny to back him in the North End wards. The Weasel is running for the at-large seat, so he needs to pick up votes wherever he can. The Calvino organization delivers, particularly in the city government primaries."

"So if it's just politics as usual, why'd he run off when he saw me?"

"You've got a bad rep, as far as the department is concerned. You and your tabloid buddy Russ have nailed the cops on a couple of occasions, right?"

"Bad cops," I said. "I'm not a crusader."

"Yeah, well it follows that Liam has a few skeletons in his closet. He must've thought you were trying to rattle his bones. Also, he doesn't need any publicity about his craven attempt to beg votes from a Mafia don. My opinion, it would probably get him as many votes as he loses, considering how popular the bad guys are in this town, but, hey, Liam is nervous. This is going to be his first run for office. If you don't count his high school election as Most Likely to be a Rodentlike Animal."

Fitzy pushed his chair back from the table. I made a grab for the tab and beat him to it.

"Your treat?" he asked. "Damn, I would have gone for the bacon and homefries."

"My best to Lois."

"Yeah," he said. "Look, I know you never take advice but I'm going to lay this on you anyhow. Keep away from Calvino. The man is dangerous."

"He could sit on me," I said.

"Hey, I'm serious. Fat Lenny is a killer. Let the cops handle this. Let Larry Sheehan take the heat, that's what he's paid for."

I said, "I'm just helping out a friend."

Fitzy sighed. "Famous last words."

The sound of a ball game in progress swept over the crowd on Lansdowne Street, directly outside Fenway Park. This was rather remarkable, since the Red Sox were on a West Coast road trip. The explanation for this apparent paradox was exceedingly simple. To quote Clarence Higgs, the production director:

"It's just noise. You know, from the park loudspeaker system? Recorded live last week and played back now. Lindy's idea. Helps get the extras in the mood. Makes 'em feel like there's a real game going on."

Higgs, who'd had all the warmth of a human snow cone in our previous encounters, was inexplicably friendly that morning. He seemed to have the impression that I had somehow "straightened out Miss Bangs," as he put it.

"Look," I said, watching the torturously slow process of organizing the crowd scene. "All we did was let her spend a few nights with us, get her out of the hotel. Whatever Lindy has or hasn't done, it's been all on her own."

Higgs smiled. "Anything you say," he said.

The scene outside Fenway Park was reasonably close to the way I'd written it: Casey chases Smilin' Stan Seigel through a street crowded with vendors and Sox fans. He's unable to fire his weapon for fear of hitting innocent civilians. Seigel, a psychopathic killer, has no such reservations. He blasts away. One of his wild shots hits the propane tank of a hot dog cart, blowing it sky high. Casey is knocked down, losing Seigel in the mob. End of scene.

Total length in the novel, three pages. Elapsed time on screen, two minutes.

"On a feature film we'd chop it to thirty seconds," Higgs told me. "For TV we can't justify the expense of extras unless it covers two minutes, minimum. Screws up the editing pace but it can't be helped."

"Uh-huh," I said, trying to sound as if I knew what he was talking about. "So how's it going?"

"Assuming the sky doesn't collapse, assuming no floods or earthquakes or unforeseen disasters, fine." His walkie-talkie sputtered. Higgs made a face and said, "'Scuse me, I have to go scream at somebody."

So much for his warmth and good humor.

Other than a polite invitation forwarded from the director, I had no particular reason to visit the location. Okay, maybe I wanted to see Lindy. Try to sort out a few things. But when I got there she was busy setting up the sequence of shots that would culminate in the detonation of the hot dog cart. She gave me a friendly, noncommittal wave and returned to her task. No time to spare for idle conversation. Or was she giving me a message? A tease is just a tease, ta dum, ta dee, to the tune of "As Time Goes By."

Just as well. What was I thinking? I loved Meg. Meg loved me. There was no place in our little script for a third party, no matter how lovely her legs. Legs that were clad, at that moment, in tight, faded denims that defined the pert curve of her buttocks as she leaned down from the boom truck to confer with the cameraman.

"You got a dirty mind. I never suspected."

I jumped. Larry Sheehan was standing behind me. Grinning and cocking his fingers at me. Gotcha.

"What are you doing here?"

"Same as you," he said, "getting an eyeful. Also I wanted a few words with my favorite wise guy."

The tape-recorded noise of the ball game ceased abruptly. Clarence Higgs raised a megaphone and announced that the first sequence was about to start shooting. All extras were to return to their marks and await the signal.

"Russ White call you?" I asked, trying to sound casual.

"Yeah. So what, am I supposed to be grateful? Huh?"

Detective Sheehan, I suddenly realized, was very pissed off.

"Hey, what's the problem?" I said. "We played a hunch and as soon as it paid off we gave you the name. Like good little citizens."

Sheehan grabbed the back of my chair and backed me up a few feet, just to demonstrate who was in charge. "I already knew about that Teresa broad, you schmuck."

"Oh, yeah?"

"You know the problem I got with you, Hawkins? You think you're so fucking smart. Only thing is when you get out on the street you do one dumb thing after another."

"I give up," I said, attempting to set the wheel brake. "Cool down, okay? You're making me nervous."

"Yeah?" He jerked my chair around, facing him. "Know what makes me nervous? Wiseguy civilians messing with professionals. Asshole reporters, they make me nervous. Huh? Am I getting through to you, Hawkins?"

"Larry, for Chrissake let go of the chair."

He backed off and lit a cigarette. Staring me down through the wisps of smoke. "For your information, asshole, we've had a line on Teresa Cotillo since before Sully disappeared."

I said, "Oh."

"That all you can say? It ever occur to you, Hawkins, that we might have an undercover setup in the North End? That we might be staking out places this lady has been known to frequent? That your presence in the area, asking questions, might throw a wrench in the works? Might even compromise the safety of my men? Huh? You got an answer for me, wise guy?"

He threw the cigarette down, stomped on it. Very impressive in a tantrum was Sergeant Detective Sheehan. I was about to make an apology, when the propane tank exploded.

CHAPTER NINETEEN

IT HAPPENED SO FAST I HAVE TO RELY ON the testimony of other eye witnesses. Missed it myself. How the hot dog cart stunt misfired, slightly injuring one of the extras, and how Sergeant Detective Lawrence Sheehan, of the elite Homicide Unit, drew his weapon and threw himself over the body of wheelchair-bound mystery author J. D. Hawkins.

That's how the *Globe* had it. They missed the dialogue.

"Larry, I didn't know you cared!"

"Aw, shaddup!" He said, holstering his weapon. "Just a reflex. These fuckin' movies. Everything's fake."

Still it was comforting to know that the man who had been roundly cussing me out was willing, at the drop of a small explosive charge, to defend me with his life.

"It's just you'd make such an easy target," he said uneasily, unwilling to make eye contact. "Don't forget, they come after Sully with a bomb the first time."

The Chelsea tough guy was embarrassed! The slight rise of color in his normally pasty-pale complexion, the hesitating speech pattern, the shifting eyes, it all added up. Sheehan was mortified.

The film crew reacted to the accident with what could only be described as tightly focused hysteria. The misfire meant a delay of at least an hour while the stunt was re-rigged. Lindy paced with the pent-up energy of a Meth-edrine addict, her eyes shifting from the stunt sequence to the sky. Worried about rain on this bluest of blue-sky mornings. Burt Bardo went to the barricades and signed autographs before returning to his trailer. Most of his fans seemed to be middle-aged women. An ambulance backed through the crowd, removing the wounded extra, who grinned hugely as they strapped him into the gurney: contemplating the prospect of a lawsuit, no doubt. Clarence Higgs communed with his walkie-talkie, eyeballing the sky, like Lindy.

The sun stayed out. The two-minute chase sequence was completed after twelve hours, just before sunset, with the aid of klieg lights. So I heard. By then I was in a different kind of trouble and my selfish concerns about the celluloid distortion of Casey were forgotten.

The situation was about to get ugly and dangerous. I had no way of knowing that, of course. I wanted to do it my way, like the song says, and no amount of persuading by Sheehan was going to change my tune.

"You need to get smart," Sheehan was saying. "Use your brain. Keep out of this and let me handle it. You think you can accomplish anything by taking to that bloated cockroach Fat Lenny? The truth never passed his lips."

"Too busy belching," I said.

That got a smile from Sheehan. Just a twitch in the deep creases, a trace element of humor. Then he was bearing down again.

"He told you, what, let me guess, this woman Teresa

is no relation? Right? Pure coincidence they got the same last name. Right?"

I nodded.

"She's a first cousin," Sheehan said, disgusted. As if merely mentioning the name Calvino stirred up his guts. "Now to a North End Italian family, a first cousin is someone who practically *lives* with you, okay? Most definitely considered an intimate part of the family. The problem with Teresa, the way a meatball like Calvino sees it, is not that she tried to get a cop killed. Pin a medal on the broad, right? The problem is she's a schizo. The lady has been hospitalized. That's like being an epileptic, or worse, in the old country. Bad blood, you get it? A form of weakness. So she's cut off. Denied access to the family. They pretend she doesn't exist."

"You're saying the Calvino mob is not involved?"

Sheehan shrugged. "Not directly. My sources tell me she went to Fat Lenny and he told her to get lost. What he didn't do was report that a known lunatic had expressed an interest in taking a cop's life. So in my book he's an accomplice, even if he's not legally culpable. If Sully don't come out of this alive I'm going after the bastard. Piss on the rules. They want my badge they can have it."

Sheehan was accompanying me to my van. I kept my pace slow, wanting to extract as much as I could while the mood was right. As we conversed, his eyes kept flitting around, picking out rooflines, doorways, shadows on the brick walls of the warehouses surrounding the ball park area.

"Why Sully?" I asked. "What made her pick on Sully?"

I wasn't sure I wanted to know the answer. I expected to be told it was somehow my fault, or Casey's fault. I had based a popular fictional character on Tim Sullivan, thus putting him in jeopardy. But Sheehan laughed. A regular guffaw.

"I love it," he said. "There's something you *don't* know. And it's so fucking *obvious*."

"Larry," I said. "I'm perfectly willing to confess my stupidity. I'll sign an affidavit to that effect if you like. Only tell me. Please?"

"This is beautiful. It's staring you right in the face. Mr. Smart Guy. Mr. Mystery Writer. Mr. Know-It-All."

"Larry? Detective Sheehan? Show a little mercy."

"Mercy? Hey, find yourself a priest, you want mercy. All I'm saying to you here is, yes, we know why this crazy broad wants to off Sully, and no, I ain't in a position to share that information with a civilian. It's under investigation."

In the distance there was a roar of approval from an imaginary crowd at an imaginary ball game. Sheehan squinted, his face creasing in a wiseguy grin. He had me.

"How about this," I said, trying a different tack. "Did George Gritz know what Leland Maddock was doing?"

"George who?"

"The publisher of *American Mercenary*."

Sheehan made a face. "Oh, him. Can't say if he knew the specifics. Damn sure he knew the magazine was being used as a clearinghouse for murder. The crazy broad Teresa wasn't the only one found it convenient to hire a hit man through the classifieds. What I heard, the feds have at least three confirmed deaths and a half-dozen attempts made by scumbags who advertised their services in that goofy rag. It's only a matter of time before an indictment comes down."

"Okay," I said. "We know about Leland Maddock. But who has she got working for her now? Who took Sully, another nut from the magazine?"

Sheehan stopped in his tracks and cocked his head. The V-shaped smile had lost all trace of humor. "We? Did I hear you say we? I'm not getting through to you, huh? Read my lips: this is not a *we* situation. Now go home and write a book or something."

CHAPTER TWENTY

THE SUN WAS SHINING ON OLD GLORY ES-
tates. The sky was blue, the lawn was green, and the tip
of the general's nose was as red as an August raspberry.
Beads of sweat dripped from the cleft in his chin. Having
just completed ten circuits of his quarter-mile, chipped-
marble track, he collapsed on the finely manicured lawn
and panted heartily until he had his breath back.

"Gets the old ticker thumping," he said, taking a
towel from Captain Beaker, who was tricked out in
freshly pressed fatigues and mirrored sunglasses. "When
the tough get going, it's because they know how to out-
run the adversary, right, Beaker?"

"That's correct, General," the captain said in his soft,
mournful way.

"Speaking of which," Gritz said. "You seem to get
around pretty good in that contraption. Healthy set of
biceps, good chest."

"I'm no athlete, General. I stay in shape because I
need the upper body strength."

"Exactly my point. We're all looking for the edge."

Gritz used the towel to burr his crew cut, then dropped it to the ground. Beaker scooped up the soiled towel. The mirrored lenses made him look like an elongated bug. A praying mantis in camouflage fatigues. Gritz sat down on a bench in a shady spot under a massive oak. I pushed through the grass, positioned my chair opposite the general, and waited. It was his magazine, his estate, his move.

He smiled and said, "When the call came in from the gate that you were requesting a visit, there was some discussion as to the advisability of allowing you access."

"Oh?"

"Captain Beaker thinks you may be a troublemaker, right Beaker?"

For once the captain did not parrot his deferential agreement. He glanced away from me, as if embarrassed.

"It's understandable he should feel that way," Gritz said amiably. "A lot of people have been making trouble for us lately. Government agents, bureaucrats, communist sympathizers, and the like."

"Journalists," Captain Beaker said, coughing into his fist.

"Same thing," Gritz said dismissively. "The upshot is that after your first visit Captain Beaker checked out your background, Mr. Hawkins. Rather extensively."

"Oh?" I said. Getting that old sinking feeling.

"We have access to certain government files. The information the files provide is not always relevant, but it can be interesting. For instance three years ago you signed a petition favoring stricter gun control in the city of Boston."

"I did?"

"According to the files."

"Probably true," I said. "I have part of a bullet in my spine. I'm inclined to favor stricter gun control."

General Gritz nodded, assessing me. "The interesting thing is that the same file also reveals that two years ago you were granted a permit to carry a concealed weapon." A tight, white grin flickered nervously. "How does that square with favoring stricter gun control?"

"It doesn't," I said. "I'm just a bundle of contradictions."

Gritz smiled again. He seemed at ease with the idea of contradictions. "You own a sidearm?"

"Sure," I said. "That's why I applied for the permit."

I didn't bother explaining that the gun had been purchased in a fit of anxiety over Megan's safety and that it was now stored in a safe deposit box on Dartmouth Street—not exactly handy, if I ever had the urge to shoot someone.

"Follow me," the general said, getting up from the bench. "I'm sure you'll be interested. Maybe you can use it in your book. If you *are* writing a book," he added with a wink.

He led, we followed. The general, yours truly, and Captain Beaker bringing up the rear. It's hard to march in a wheelchair but I did my best. Hup-one-two. Push-three-four. Glide-five-six.

I'll say this for Gorgeous George. He wasn't embarrassed by wealth, or afraid to display it. Old Glory Estates had all the amenities big money could buy. Riding stables, putting greens, indoor and outdoor swimming pools, greenhouses to supply the formal gardens. Shooting range. All courtesy of the Gritz vacuum tube and the sacred rites of inheritance.

The shooting range was a long, neatly trimmed building of white clapboard. I must have been in an irreverant mood because the cedar shingled roof reminded me of the general's haircut—stubby and stiff and somewhat pointed.

"We try to test all the products advertised in our publications," Gritz explained, holding the door as I wheeled into the padded silence of the building, "partly because we consider it our responsibility to do so, but mostly because it's a lot of goddamn good fun."

Captain Beaker turned on the lights and unlocked the armory, which was secured by a sliding, roll-down door of the type favored by retailers in borderline neighborhoods. It was like watching a new store open. *Guns-R-Us*. I was impressed.

"What's that thing?" I asked, pointing. "Looks like a rocket launcher."

Gritz chuckled. "That's because it *is* a rocket launcher. The Stinger, shoulder mounted, heat seeking. Turns an enemy aircraft into fairy dust in eight seconds. Weapon of choice for freedom fighters the world over."

"You can *own* something like that?"

"I'm a collector, Mr. Hawkins. I have the necessary permits. And of course the warhead isn't armed."

"Of course."

The Stinger rocket was simply the largest item of a vast collection of military hardware. General Gritz had a particular fondness for automatic and semiautomatic weapons. Submachine guns. He called them SMGs.

"Your SMG has a proud history," he explained, hefting a Thompson Model 1921 fitted with a 50-round drum. "The original Tommy gun, conceived by General John Thompson in World War I. The idea was to make the machine gun portable enough to use in close-range trench warfare. It worked beautifully. It was Al Capone who gave it the romantic connotation, though."

I said, "Excuse me, romantic?"

"Love at first sight," Gritz said. He tossed the heavy

weapon to Captain Beaker, who returned it to the shelf. "You want to talk modern romance, we have the MP5-SD. Isn't it a beauty?"

"Gorgeous," I said doubtfully.

"Heckler & Koch with an internal suppressor. Choice of SWAT teams everywhere. Quick, quiet, won't disturb the neighbors. Course, if you want *real* silence in an SMG—your basic counterterrorist weapon—then you'd have to go for the Uzi with a Ciener suppressor. Sounds like a cat purring."

Gritz had a weapon in each hand. He was careful to avert the barrels, but the effect was still unsettling.

"I thought those things were illegal," I said.

"Not if you have the right connections," Gritz said with a sneaky grin. "Not if you know the right spooks."

"Spooks?"

"A certain government agency," Gritz said. "You can guess which one."

"Sir," Beaker interrupted. "Do you think it's wise to—"

"At ease, Captain. It's not exactly a state secret that we received a federal grant to conduct a comparative analysis study of SMG efficiency. And that we are duly licensed to do so," he said. "Fact of the matter is, Mr. Hawkins, it was the subject of a feature in our August issue. Right, Beaker?"

The captain sighed. "Yes, sir. It was indeed, sir."

"You see, Mr. Hawkins, I want to be candid with you."

"Great," I said. "So tell me about Leland Maddock."

Silence. You could have heard an Uzi purr. General Gritz shook his head and returned the SMGs to the shelf. Clearly I had disappointed him.

"Aren't you even going to say 'Leland who?'" I asked.

Gritz slipped his hands in his pockets and leaned

against the armory counter. The military genius at ease. "Few weeks ago I might have. Then that fool Maddock tried to terminate a homicide detective. A friend of yours, correct?"

"Correct."

"And if I'm not mistaken this same homicide detective is now missing and presumed dead?"

"I'm not presuming that, General."

Gritz stirred uneasily. "Well, missing then. I heard about it, of course. Captain Beaker started tracking the story when Leland's name came up. So to anticipate your next question, Mr. Hawkins, yes, Leland Maddock worked here. Briefly. In the capacity of groundskeeper. He had rather unpredictable work habits, however, and we had to let him go."

"Groundskeeper?" I said. "You must have been aware that Maddock wanted to be a soldier of fortune. He was obsessed with the idea."

"He did mention something about that, yes."

"And he ran an ad in your classified section."

Now it was Captain Beaker who sighed. "General, sir, I request that you terminate this interview."

The choice of the word *terminate* was disturbing but Gritz merely nodded. "I'll just say this, Mr. Hawkins. The same thing I told the boys from the FBI. I have always assumed that any man using our classified section to advertise his availability as a mercenary is seeking a paramilitary position. I was never aware that a few disturbed individuals used our ads to arrange murders-for-hire. As I'm sure you're aware, there are a number of civil lawsuits pending. My lawyers—and Captain Beaker, of course—have advised me not to comment."

"So you won't tell me who hired Leland Maddock? Or where that person might be found?"

"General," Beaker said in a warning tone.

"Look, General, I'm pretty sure it was a woman named Teresa Cotillo. Ring any bells? If we can locate her we may find Lieutenant Sullivan. If it's not too late."

"There'll be no comment," Beaker said.

Gritz waved him off. "Hawkins, I never heard of this Cotillo woman. I had no idea she hired Leland Maddock. Leland was a psycho. A nut. As soon as we realized our mistake we dismissed him."

"I'm not interested in assigning blame, General," I said, fibbing slightly. "I just want to know where Teresa is hiding."

"Sorry," Gritz said. "Can't help you there. Would if I could."

He decided to direct the conversation back to the original topic. Firepower. "Beaker," he said, "the new Roltner please."

With a notable lack of enthusiasm Captain Beaker produced a slim designer briefcase from the armory. The type of briefcase high-powered executives carry to impress other high-powered executives. Gritz smiled to himself as he dialed the combination and snapped open the lid.

Inside was an item that looked like no handgun I had ever seen. Gritz handed it to me. I hefted the thing. Obviously it was not a real weapon. A stage prop, or something out of "Star Trek."

"Plastic," I said. "Can't weigh more than a few ounces."

He nodded. "High-stress plastic. Fires single action, a three-slug burst, or full automatic."

"You mean it's real?"

He looked surprised. "Of course it's real. The first all-plastic machine pistol. It's a .233 caliber with a 60-round clip. Nonmetallic slugs, of course."

I looked on, amazed, as he produced a plastic ammunition clip. He snapped out one of the bullets. It was, as he promised, plastic. Shell casing and slug, both plastic. Amazing. The rim of the shell was coated with a thin copper foil.

"No firing pin," he explained, slipping the magazine into the pistol. "That's the beauty of it. Shells detonated by a piezoelectric charge. Same as a cigarette lighter. Damned expensive of course, but you'd expect that of the ultimate concealed weapon."

"You could carry that thing through an airport metal detector," I said.

"That's the idea," he agreed. "Beaker? Target please. Let's show Mr. Hawkins the magic of modern technology, shall we?"

"Yes, sir."

Beaker manipulated a control, activating a target. It was a full-size human silhouette, drawn rapidly forward by an overhead cable. General Gritz dropped to one knee, braced the plastic machine pistol against his right shoulder, and twisted the forward grip of the gun. It sounded like someone coughing discreetly, but the spray of bullets instantly reduced the target to so much confetti.

Gritz got to his feet. There was a slight sheen of sweat on his forehead. His eyes were bright. "Tell *that* to the marines," he said, grinning. "Right, Beaker?"

"Yes, sir," Beaker said without enthusiasm. "Right."

"Captain Beaker thinks the Roltner is unreliable," Gritz explained. "He doesn't understand that plastics are the future."

Gritz turned as he spoke. Lucky for me he had the machine pistol pointing down. Not lucky for him, because for no reason at all the gun of the future fired a three-slug burst, neatly removing a toe from the general's right foot.

"Shit," he groaned as the blood drained from his face.

He dropped the gun. It went off again. Slugs exploded along the concrete floor. Captain Beaker danced. For a mournful man he was very nimble on his feet. Graceful, almost.

He had to be very careful. She would fly into a rage if she found out he was bringing water to the injured man. Water, and this time some fruit and cheese he had taken from the rectory kitchen.

At the bottom of the stairs he paused, his massive head cocked. Looking, listening. Teresa was not at her altar. The candles had burned out and the darkness was nearly absolute. He felt his way along the damp walls until he came to the small alcove where the injured man was kept.

He paused just inside the alcove, listening again. He heard the faint rasping noise of the injured man breathing. Good. While there was breath there was life. Carefully he inched his way along the floor.

"Water," a voice croaked.

He made reassuring noises. Yes there would be water. Water and fruit and cheese. Enough to sustain life.

Teresa wanted the injured man to go with her angels. She wanted death and vengeance. But after a life of pain and injury, he couldn't stand to see anything hurt. Not even a man.

He knelt, located the parched, feverish lips of the injured man, and presented him with a cup of water.

"Drink," the big man muttered. "Live."

CHAPTER TWENTY-ONE

WHEN I LEFT THE GENERAL HE WAS ALMOST incoherent with pain. The Roltner had been sabotaged, he raged. It was the work of anarchists, Communists, Democrats.

"They want to break my spirit," he grimaced. "Never! Never!"

An ambulance driver was arguing with the security guard as I drove through the checkpoint. It was a red ambulance, which may have explained the delay.

This time I found Route 128 without any problems and drove south on Route 1, back into the smoke. Heading for the North End of the city, where all roads seemed to lead. If I hadn't been concentrating on the priest and how he might help I might have noticed that the highway was paved with good intentions.

Father Fabrizzi was in the rectory garden, reading a paperback romance novel. The cover was slightly lurid, which may explain why he hastily closed the book and put it face down on the bench when he heard my wheels crunching over the gravel. The bench was situated under the pear tree. The leaves were beginning to turn. It made a pretty, peaceful picture, if you didn't happen to notice the overripe tomatoes rotting on the plants and the unplucked weeds clotting the garden.

"*Buon giorno*, Father," I said.

The priest's mild brown eyes regarded me with alarm. He looked around as if measuring the fastest line of retreat from the little courtyard, then seemed to change his mind.

"Good day," he said, adding, "You speak Italian?"

I shook my head. "Just being polite. I take it you remember me?"

He smiled. His close-shaven beard showed through pale, translucent skin like a layer of faint blue dust. "Of course. You came looking for a friend. A policeman, I believe. Has he been found?"

"Not yet" I said, halting my chair in the center of the gravel path.

"I'm sorry for his troubles."

"Sure you are," I said.

The priest brought his hands together and sighed. "How can we help you today, Mr. Hawkins? Another matter of life and death, I suppose?"

"The same one," I said. "Her name is Teresa. Maiden name Calvino. Fat Lenny's crazy cousin."

"Ah," he said. "That one."

"Been around lately?"

The priest studied his nails, head bowed. His ears were so thin and white they might have been sculpted from candle wax. He looked up, assuming the forthright manner of a man who had made a decision.

When he spoke I couldn't help but notice that his English had improved considerably. It was either a miracle of syntax, or he'd been using his accent to help cover the lies of omission he'd fed me that first day in the garden.

"Insanity comes in many forms," he said. "Did you know that many of the saints were considered insane by those who persecuted them? Saint Francis for example?"

"But not Saint Teresa," I said.

He glanced away. "No," he said. "Perhaps not."

"I'm just an ignorant layman, Father. Tell me, did any of these misunderstood saints attempt murder? Or arrange abductions?"

He sighed and fiddled with the paperback. "You must understand that Teresa is a very confused person. Easily influenced. The illness . . ."

"What about the illness, Father?"

He looked disgruntled. "The psychologists have names for everything," he said, waving a hand dismissively. "They wish to turn faith into an element of science. Like a thing made in a beaker, or examined under a microscope. Teresa hears voices, therefore she is a schizophrenic. It is a weak argument, no?"

"You have another diagnosis?"

Fabrizzi shook his head impatiently. "It is not a matter simply of diagnosis. Was Mary a delusional psychopath, tormenting Joseph? Was the Immaculate Conception a kind of hysterical pregnancy? Was Joan of Arc a schizophrenic? Can we fairly judge spiritual matters by psychiatric terms?"

Answering a direct question with another question. It was a form of torture I'd had to endure in catechism, those interminable Saturday mornings in the basement classroom at Saint Luke's.

"Joan of Arc was fighting a religious war," I countered. "She wasn't trying to have a cop killed."

"You're wrong about Teresa," the priest said. "She wouldn't hurt anyone. Others have taken advantage."

"Which others, Father? Can you give me any names?"

He stared at his nails again. I had the distinct impression that he was playing a waiting game. As if he expected help to arrive. Not that I could have prevented him from leaving the garden.

"You know one of them already," he said. "The violent man the police shot."

"Leland Maddock?"

He nodded. "An ugly person. No better than an animal. He took what little money she had."

"I know about Maddock, although I'm not sure who took advantage of whom. Did you actually meet him?"

"No, but Teresa described him."

"I see. And based on her description, you decided that he was taking advantage of her. Did you know she paid him to plant a bomb in Detective Sullivan's car?"

He said, "No, of course not. And I'm sure the bomb was his idea. Teresa is not a killer. She is sometimes . . . confused."

"You said that already, Father," I said, wheeling closer. "I didn't believe it the first time. Not as an excuse. The woman made threats. Ugly threats. We assume she made contact with a self-styled mercenary. Your precious Teresa may not be rational, but she sure as hell is dangerous."

His chin bobbed up. "I disagree."

"Where is she, Father? Are you hiding her here?"

He looked startled. "Of course not."

"Where can I find her, Father?"

He shrugged. "Teresa comes and she goes. I have not asked where she hides. I am here only to give her consolation."

"And to hear her confession?"

He stiffened. "That is between us. And God, of course."

"Of course."

"I cannot help you, Mr. Hawkins."

I shook my head. "Come on, Father. You can help. I don't know if Teresa is legally insane, though I assume she is. At the very least she needs to be confined."

An expression of disgust mottled the pale skin. A nerve had been touched. "Have you ever visited an insane asylum, Mr. Hawkins? No? They are horrible places. My own mother . . ." He cleared his throat. A vein pulsed in his temple. "Teresa could not survive. In the asylum she would die, or take her own life."

I decided to try a different tack. Feed him a lie and see how he'd react. "Fat Lenny said you wanted to have her committed."

The dark, somber eyes flashed with anger. "He lies! I asked him to help her. To see that she was taken back into the bosom of her family. He . . . he *laughed*. Accused me of having lustful desires. Me! Who wanted only to protect her!"

Passion. It was there just beneath the surface, waiting to burst forth. I had no idea what demons tormented Teresa, but Fabrizzi's motivations were becoming clear.

"You love her," I said.

He opened his mouth to speak, thought better of it.

"Father, listen to me. If she turns herself in she may get the help she needs. If they find she's killed a cop all bets are off. Cop killers end up doing hard time, Father. Sometimes they end up dead."

He shook his head.

"And if the cops don't get her I've got a feeling Fat Lenny will. Teresa's a troublemaker. And he has his own way of handling troublemakers."

"But she's of his blood! He wouldn't dare."

I laughed. Wanting to rub it in, make him react. "Get serious, Father. You think Calvino really cares about family? He'd strangle his own mother to save himself a day in jail. Forget the Godfather routine. That's only in the movies."

But the priest wasn't listening. He was tuning me out, focusing on the paperback lying next to him. Losing himself in a world where the purity of love always triumphs. In the autumn light he looked, at that moment, like a pale, ascetic Romeo in the ruins of his garden, waiting to embrace the soul of his mad Juliet.

CHAPTER TWENTY-TWO

IT WAS THE GARDEN THAT GAVE IT AWAY, OF course. The garden that had been so meticulously maintained by the broken-down, nearly mute prizefighter. But in the week or so since I'd been there the weeds had taken over. Tomatoes had been left to rot on the vines. Leaves were unraked.

Where was Kid Tony? What had compelled him to abandon the small sanctuary that had seemed, at the time, to be his life's work?

Pondering this, and somewhat under the spell of romantic passion that the priest had radiated—how the poor man had yearned for the impossible!—I rolled right on by the public telephone at the corner grocery. Thereby missing an opportunity to act on a vague impulse to contact Detective Sheehan.

Larry hadn't mentioned Kid Tony. Did he know about Torelli's connection to the priest, the parish, the streets of the old neighborhood? Maybe I'd been imagining the gentleness I sensed in the big man. Maybe the haunted look was no more than a reflection of emptiness within. An echo from the ruined chapel of a bruised and battered mind.

In the clearing stands a boxer.

The line of that old pop tune teased me. Where had I last seen Kid Tony? Not in a clearing, surely. Clearings were in short supply in the North End. I halted my chair and looked around, searching for a glimmer that would spark my memory. Blacktop. Brick tenement buildings. Blue sky, fading rapidly as the sun hurried down.

A vacant lot. No, not quite vacant. The ruins of a small, burned-out church. All gone save for a rusted iron fence, the stone arch of a doorway, and a few crumbling walls. I had seen Kid Tony standing under that arch of stone. He'd been waiting for me there. Waiting to speak a few halting words.

My cop friend, he'd said. *Gone to Heaven.*

I'd forgotten that Kid Tony had gone out of his way to ask me if I had known his unnamed friend. A dead cop. That was before Russ White and I stumbled on the Paul Cotillo story, and Kid Tony had been so befuddled and confused it had never really registered before. Had he been referring to Paul Cotillo? Did he, like Father Fabrizzi, have a connection to the widow Teresa?

My cop friend.

Check it out, I thought. When all else fails rely on instinct.

But it couldn't have been instinct that made me push along the rutted sidewalk, heading for the charred ruins located a few blocks from Father Fabrizzi's church. Instinct is supposed to save you. Instinct should have returned me to the public telephone.

Curiosity, that's what it must have been. Me and the damned cat.

The arch of the vacant doorway framed a curve of darkening sky. Below, I could see that much of the church cellar remained intact. Massive floor timbers supported rectangles of weathered plywood, as if there had once been some thought given to rebuilding the structure. A portion of the vestry was similarly boarded up. Ragged tarpaulins covered a small section of roof that had survived the fire.

I rolled over a narrow walkway of poured concrete, heading for the vestry ruins. Tiny flowers had sprouted through the cracks. Wild, pretty things that mocked the adjacent destruction.

A warped piece of plywood covered the old vestry door. The open jaws of a rusty padlock hung from the hasp. I positioned my chair as near to the door as I dared and pulled it open. The hinges worked smoothly. As if recently oiled. A stairway dropped into the darkness of the cellar.

"Antonio," I called. "Kid Tony? Anybody down there?"

I shaded my eyes, trying to penetrate the shadows below. I set the wheel brakes, not wanting to slip over the edge. From where I sat it looked like the stairs went down a long way. Forever, maybe. After a minute or so I realized the darkness was not absolute. There was a faintness, a kind of flickering quality to it, as if the shadows had a life of their own.

What a crazy idea.

"Tony Torelli," I said, a little louder this time. "Is that you?"

Something moved down there. The shadows began to shift. Then the bottom stair disappeared. Impossible. I blinked and then discerned a human form advancing up-wards, cutting off the stairs with his bulk. Taking his time about it.

Kid Tony's head emerged from the shadows. That massive, battered skull with the steel-wool hair, scar-tissue nose, and quiet, bloodshot eyes. A trick of the light made it seem as if his head floated, independent of body. John the Baptist on a night-black mirror.

"You," he said.

His voice was even more jagged and damaged than I remembered. Every broken part of him had healed badly, time and again, until there was nothing left but thickened scars and bone and sinew. He lumbered up another few steps and I saw that he had on the same farmer-style coveralls he'd worn while tending the parish garden.

"Tony," I said. "I need your help."

The impassive eyes focused. Registering interest, it seemed to me.

"It's Paulie's wife," I said. "She's in big trouble. We have to find her, okay?"

"Teresa," he said.

There was a reverence in the way he pronounced the name that made me want to unlock my brakes and back the hell out of there. It was just a silly impulse. I never had the chance to act on it because a pair of iron claws suddenly gripped me around the ribs and lifted me straight out of my chair.

Had I been able to breathe I might have demanded to be put down. As it was his powerful hands cut off my air. The sensation of being suddenly removed from the wheelchair produced a spasm of pure, naked fear. My heart stuttered. I wanted to cry. Didn't only because I was too frightened.

Vertigo. I was falling. Out of control.

No, not falling. Being transported down, rapidly. When the first thrill of panic abated it became apparent that Kid Tony had thrown me over his broad shoulders. With my arms pinned I was about as threatening as a sack of grain. Blinded by the dank, waxy darkness and carried down, down, down.

Then thrown. No, not thrown, exactly. Dropped down. I could feel a damp, cold wall against my back, a solid concrete floor under my hips. The flickering was from a candle. I couldn't judge how far away it was. Might have been miles, or inches. Then it moved, came nearer. The flame doubled, reflected in the boxer's eyes. He bent down low, close enough so I could feel his breath on my face. Close enough so I could almost detect the faint heat of the flame.

"Don't move," he said.

Don't move! What a joke. Did he think my wheelchair was a fake? I wanted to ask him, taunt him, but my voice didn't seem to be functioning.

"Wait for the lady," he said. "Teresa knows."

Teresa knows? What did she know? That I couldn't move? That without my wheels under me I was as panic-stricken as a fish out of water?

In a flash all my fear and anxiety condensed into anger. I lashed out. My fingernails raked the fabric of his overalls. There was just that one touch before he and the candle disappeared. The stairs creaked under his weight, and then silence.

I shouted. I raged. I screamed. Trying to illuminate the dark with noise. After a few minutes I'd shouted myself hoarse.

Save your breath, Hawkins, my inner voice advised.

Then I heard it. A noise in the dark. A soft scuttling noise.

*   *   *

The first thing I did was try to get away. Instinct again. When something goes bump in the dark instinct tries to take control. It made me want to run. Instinct didn't care about my paraplegia. It wanted legs. Being paralyzed was no excuse. The best I could do was wiggle my hips and shift along the damp floor. Trying to pinpoint the source of the sound so I could get as far away as possible.

The sound was furtive. Sneaky. Feral. I expected to see small yellow eyes glowing in the dark.

Get a grip on yourself, Hawkins. It's only a cat or a rat.

Trouble is when you're stuck at ground level in the dark in a strange place there's no such thing as "only a rat." What made it worse was the realization that small teeth might be working on my feet and I wouldn't even feel it. I slipped my hands under my knees and pulled my legs up against my chest.

Just checking.

I listened again. Really listened. The scuttling noise was coming from one particular direction. After a while I decided the sound was not so much furtive as helpless. I pictured an animal thrashing in a trap. Immobilized. Like me.

Then the sound changed. The scuttling stopped. It spoke.

"Ack." It said. "Ack."

The voice was human.

The scuttling sound resumed.

I began to inch in that direction. Toward the sound, not away. To hell with instinct. It was slow going until I got the rhythm. Push up and lean forward. Reposition the hands. Push up and lean. Push up. Breaststroke on a sea of concrete.

Now there were two scuttling sounds. Whatever it was in the dark and myself. The sound of my legs dragging.

"Ack," It said.

Gasping. Now I was close enough to hear it breathe. It sounded weak, wounded. I kept on. Cakewalking on my palms. Getting some momentum. And bumped head first into a solid object.

Stars.

The surprise of it was worse than the jolt of pain. So much for personal radar. I listened. The scuttling was now slightly behind me. I'd gone right by. I felt my way along the wall I'd crashed into and came to an open space. A doorway.

"Ack."

I pulled myself through the opening. Something raked across my hand. I stopped. It scuttled over my hand again. I grabbed it.

A shoe. The heel had made the scuttling sound. Gingerly I touched an ankle, a trouser cuff, a thin, bony leg. The leg moved, feeble and weak.

I crawled alongside the body. Crunching glass under my hand. A pair of broken glasses.

"Sully? Is it you?"

"Jack," he muttered. "Dreamed it. Shouts."

CHAPTER TWENTY-THREE

"DREAMED IT," HE MUTTERED. "JACK SHOUT-ing."

"It's not a dream, Sully. I'm right here."

He ignored me and went on babbling about dreams and shouts. My elbow banged into a piece of crockery. It was a plate. A lump of wax was stuck to it. A guttered-out candle.

It was like finding money. I wasted a couple of precious minutes sweeping my fingers over the floor area, looking for matches. Found a jug of water, a stale sandwich wrapped in wax paper. Found matches, finally, right in my pants pocket where they'd been all along.

In the flickering light Sully looked ghastly. Blood was caked from the top of his head to the line of his jaw, and fresh blood was oozing from a wound on his temple. The side of his face was swollen to about twice normal size. One eyelid was glued shut with clotted blood. I probed gingerly, trying to assess the damage, expecting to find a bullet wound.

"Have you been shot?" I asked. He continued to ignore me. I wasn't really there. After a while I realized, with great relief, that there was no bullet wound. He'd been bludgeoned or punched.

I felt for his pulse, found it. It seemed unsteady, as if his heart was skipping beats or missing them altogether. That was scary. But what really bothered me was that the pupil of his good eye remained dilated even when I brought the candle close.

"I think you've got a concussion," I said. "A bad one, this time."

"Dreams," he said. "Shouts."

"You hang on," I instructed him. "I'll get help."

Sully mumbled something and drifted off into delirium. Hadn't understood anything I'd said. It was probable that he had no idea where he was or even what had happened to him. I went through his pockets. No gun, no badge, no wallet. And yet the candle, water, and scraps of food indicated that he hadn't merely been beaten and robbed. He was being kept alive.

Why?

Forget it, Hawkins. This is no time to ponder life's little mysteries. Time to get help. Time to make a move.

Make a move? Well, why not? Like most paraplegics, I routinely exercised, building up arm and shoulder muscles, strengthening my upper limbs to compensate for the lower. All the workouts had tangible results in terms of relative mobility. When showing off for Megan I liked to hoist my chin up to the bar one-handed. See what a hunk you've agreed to marry! How about those deltoids, babe! Silly macho stuff, perhaps, but the result is that I can get myself in and out of the wheelchair with relative ease. With grace, I like to think.

So I knew I could hoist myself up the cellar stairs, if only I could locate the damn things. I decided to leave the candle with Sully. Cold comfort, maybe, but it would be awkward trying to drag it along with me. I found my way back through the door opening—was I under the old vestry? The nave? Where?—and tried to orient myself. When I had a fix, or thought I did, I took a few deep breaths and experimented. Hefting my weight on my hands and wrists and swinging my hips along apeman fashion. Dragging my useless legs.

Attaboy, Tarzan. Get moving. Faster now, you don't know when your old pal Kid Tony will return. Might be minutes, might be hours. Go on, you can do it.

That's the kind of mental pep talk you engage in when hauling yourself over a damp cellar floor in the dark. It got me as far as another concrete wall. Good. I'd traversed the width of the cellar. Putting my back to the wall I inched along sideways. After a few miles of that I came to another opening. Tentatively I reached into the open space. My fingertips encountered something rough and solid. Wood, worn smooth on the leading edge.

A stair tread. My heart started trip-hammering. Maybe Kid Tony had left my wheelchair there at the top of the stairs. If I could just get to it I could flee into the street, calling for help. Make a scene, anything to attract attention.

It was a powerful fantasy. I could almost feel the chair under me as I bumped backwards up the stairs. Moving with the kind of hurried speed that would leave nasty bruises on my lower back and hips. No matter. Anything to escape the darkness.

To be truthful I wanted to see daylight as badly as I wanted to help Sully. And when I got to the top step, there it was. A thin, vertical line of light marked the door. I could feel myself grinning in the dark as I leaned forward and pushed.

176

The door did not budge. The padlock, the damned padlock!

I had a new curse for each tread as I bumped myself back down into the cellar. Sinking back into the darkness. The idea was to find something I could use as a pry bar. The best tactic seemed to be to get on my belly, waving my arms wide as I crawled. I turned up cans and bottles and gritty chunks of wood. Charred stuff with no strength. Debris that had spilled in as the burning church collapsed into the cellar.

What I wanted was a strip of metal thin enough to wedge into the crack of the door. Was that too much to ask? I could imagine it there, almost glowing in the dark. A cold, lovely piece of steel! Come to papa. I kept reaching and not finding. Coming up empty. I knew it was there, though. Had to be. Any minute I'd find it, get back up the stairs, pry the door open, and get the hell away. Bring back help for Sully.

It was a nice little dream while it lasted. Then the padlock snapped open. Heavy footsteps on the treads. A pool of light skittered over the cellar and quickly settled on me.

Kid Tony, equipped with a flashlight.

"No crawl away," he said gravely.

He trained the light directly in my eyes and grabbed me by the shirt collar. Dragged me back to where he'd first propped me against the wall. I punched at his legs. It was like connecting with hardened tree stumps.

"Quiet now," he ordered. "We wait for the lady."

He backed out of range, keeping the light on me. I heard a match flare. Then gradually the light began to change. At first I couldn't discern what was happening. Then it became apparent that Kid Tony was lighting candles. Lots of candles. As the dimness receded, more and more of the cellar became visible. I didn't like what I saw there, not one bit.

"Pretty," the big man said.

It was spooky. The kind of spooky that prickles the hairs on the back of your neck and sends an electric shiver down your spine. Insane spooky.

"Pretty," he said again. As if expecting me to agree.

Some of the candles were arranged on an altar. A real church altar scorched black by the fire. A filthy dark cloth covered the altar, stained with rusty-colored splotches that looked, to my semiprofessional eye, like dried blood. A cross rose behind the altar, similarly blackened. I could make out a lighter patch where the figure of Christ had been removed. Nailed in its place, or rather thumbtacked, were a number of photographs. I couldn't quite make out the images. Wasn't at all sure I wanted to, for that matter. I'm not exactly the religious type, but the thing radiated a malicious blasphemy that would have chilled the stoniest of nonbelievers.

Kid Tony didn't feel that way, though.

"Pretty," he sighed. It was like a prayer or an invocation. He crouched, holding himself utterly still, as if rooted. In the flickering candlelight he looked as if he'd been carved from stone with a very dull chisel. Beyond him I could just make out the alcove where Sully lay. He didn't appear to be moving.

"Very nice," I said, trying to sound agreeable. "But it would be even nicer if you'd go get some help. That man over there is very sick. He needs to be in a hospital."

"Quiet," Kid Tony rumbled. "Wait for the lady."

The candles were everywhere. Perched around the altar, scattered on the shallow steps below it, on the floor, strewn along some of the fallen timbers, everywhere. The odor of burning wax quickly became thick and cloying. I thought of the myriad candles in the squalid room where Leland Maddock had lived. Had this place inspired his bizarre attempts at interior decoration? Was madness a virus that flourished in candlelight?

It was a crazy idea. An idea almost as scary as the altar and the cross. I tried to push it out of my head. No room in there for crazy ideas.

Kid Tony shuffled into the alcove—it had the look of having once been a coal bin—and crouched next to Sully. His touch was gentle, almost nurturing. Sully moved, muttered, fell back unconscious. The big man remained crouched for a while, watching him sleep.

When he emerged from the alcove he faced the blackened altar and knelt. He touched his forehead, his heart, each shoulder. Making the sign of the cross. He heaved himself to his feet and approached the altar. That was when I first noticed the tabernacle. It too had been scorched, blending into the dark background. Tony slid open the little port and removed a couple of objects. Then he came to me with the stuff cupped in his palms.

He held his hands out. "Friend?" he asked.

What he had stored in the tabernacle was a .38 Smith & Wesson revolver, standard issue, and a detective shield. Sully's gun and Sully's shield.

"Friend?" he asked again.

"Right," I said. "Those belong to my friend."

I was calculating that the revolver was just within reach. Should I try for it? I gave it away by shifting a little too soon and Tony instantly withdrew his hands. He slipped his index finger into the trigger guard, cocked the hammer, and pulled the trigger.

Click.

"Hide bullets," he said.

"Good idea," I said. "Hiding the bullets is always a good idea."

He nodded gravely, studying me. "Friend hurt bad," he said. "Head busted."

"Help us," I asked. "If he doesn't go to a hospital soon he'll die. Go get the priest, Tony. Get Father Fabrizzi."

He shook his head. "Teresa say no."

"Where is she?" I asked. "Where is this Teresa?"

He ignored me and returned the gun and shield to the tabernacle. An acolyte from a nightmare, tending a blasphemed host. The way he hovered around the candles, checking out the flames, convinced me that he was drawn more to the soft, flickering lights than to the ruined altar. It was the candles that were pretty.

This time he returned with a piece of paper. An article torn from the *Boston Standard*. It was Russ White's profile of Detective Timothy Sullivan. The newsprint photo of Sully was smeared, slightly out of focus, and paired with a studio portrait of Burt Bardo.

"Friend hurt Paulie," Kid Tony informed me.

"Paulie hurt himself."

"No, no," he said, as if instructing a child. "Man hurt Paulie. Very bad man."

He moved away again, tending the candles. While he played in his little garden of wax I tried to recall if I'd let anybody know where I was going. Not Sheehan, I'd blown that chance. How about Fitzy? We'd discussed Father Fabrizzi, surely. Or was that wishful thinking? On recollection it seemed that Fitzy had devoted most of his energy to dissecting the character, or lack of it, of Liam "The Weasel" Delaney. Meg? I might have mentioned the need to check out the priest. Or maybe not. In any event she wouldn't be home until five or so. How late would I have to be before Meg started worrying? How long before she reported me missing?

So far I had a list of questions and no answers. Pleading with Kid Tony hadn't worked. It was time to try something more dramatic.

So I started to choke. At first I covered my mouth, as if ashamed of a bad cough. Then I let it get a little worse. *Hack hack.* I had to crank it up before Tony took any notice. When I had his attention I moved my hands to my throat and pressed. Cut off the circulation a little and your eyes will bug out. This is very effective in restaurants when the waiters ignore you. Kid Tony didn't seem particularly impressed though.

"Doc-tor!" I gasped. "Dying!"

The big son of a bitch poked me with his foot. I fell over on my side and commenced to flop around. Faking a seizure. "Priest!" I gasped. "Get . . . me . . . priest!"

It's not easy to look beseeching when your eyes are bugging out. I gave it the old college try. Kid Tony finally showed some concern. I tried to talk while inhaling, an interesting effect, and kept mouthing the word *priest* like a wounded foxhole buddy in a Spencer Tracy movie. I had to keep this up until I really *did* have a coughing fit before the big lug took action.

I didn't dare turn as he limped away. Best to keep up the quivers and the coughing. I heard him ascending the stairs though, and there was no doubt about it when he clicked shut the padlock.

The damned padlock.

So much for Plan A, Escape from the Dungeon. The alternative was Plan B, Waiting for the Priest. I was kidding myself, of course. Convinced by my own performance. I should have known better. No one had ever followed one of my scripts, so why expect Kid Tony to be any different?

He returned quicker than I'd expected. As soon as I heard the padlock unsnap I started dying again. Wheezing and groaning. *Hack hack, ugh ugh.* Face averted from the stairway so I didn't have to bother with making my eyes bug out. I heard two sets of footsteps approaching, one heavier, the other light. When I detected the scent of incense my heart gladdened.

Someone knelt over me. A soft voice whispered, "Are you dead yet?"

I jerked around. A black-haired witch grinned at me as smoke poured from a censer.

CHAPTER TWENTY-FOUR

SHE WAS A BEAUTY, NO DOUBT ABOUT IT. Wearing a black dress draped from neck to ankles. Big dark eyes, thick black hair, strong white teeth. Lovely full lips, if you ignored what came out of them.

"Dirty beast," she said, holding the smoking censer so close I began to choke in earnest. "Go ahead and die!"

I tried to grab the censer chain. She screamed and slapped me in the face. Hard enough so that flecks of light whirled before my eyes. The lady could punch.

"They sent you here," she hissed, wrapping a black knit shawl tight around her shoulders. "You came to desecrate this place."

The place had already been thoroughly desecrated but there was no point in trading insults. Not with Kid Tony standing by, his big fists clenched.

The woman who had been born Teresa Calvino remained crouched, her hands splayed out over the floor, her head cocked at an odd angle. "Oh, yeah?" she announced in a sing-song voice. "Who told you that? Go 'way, leave us alone. . . . Don't you see the candles? Candles, ha! Scared you, didn't we!"

The thing of it is, she wasn't talking to me. Teresa was responding to voices in her head. The one-sided conversation continued, with pauses that indicated she was hearing a response.

"Paulie didn't say any such thing. . . . You're trying to trick me but I have the power. All I have to do is make the sign and you'll disappear. That what you want? . . . Go on, get back!" She lunged, raising a fist at her invisible tormentors.

I felt sick. There would be no reasoning with the lady. Making nice talk with a schizophrenic in full thrall of madness is about as effective as spitting into a hurricane.

"They're gone," she said, suddenly calm. "Antonio, light more candles."

She then gaped, as if sighting me for the first time. "Go away," she said, covering her eyes with her hands and peering at me from between her fingers. "You can't fool me."

It's more than a little disconcerting to be mistaken for a hallucination. I tried to look and sound normal, or at least real, whatever *that* is. "Teresa, please listen. That man in there is badly hurt," I said, indicating the alcove where Sully lay. "He needs help. He needs a doctor."

She edged closer, giving no indication that she understood. "I know you, she said, sounding almost normal. "You're the man in the wheelchair. The story teller. The liar."

In a tight spot Peter denied his faith and his friend. Confronted by the glittering eyes of madness, I did not hesitate to deny my profession.

"You're mistaken," I said. "You've confused me with someone else. Another guy in a wheelchair."

Teresa laughed. It was not a pretty sound, not the

laugh of someone who could be reasoned with, not even close. "More lies," she said. "They come from your mouth like worms. They shot you, took away your legs, and still you seek their favor."

She had a point. Why did I continue to seek the approval, or at least the respect, of certain Boston cops, notably Sully and to a lesser extent Larry Sheehan? Was I making amends for stealing parts of them to use in my books?

I shook my head. Teresa was confusing me with her smoky madness. All that mattered was that a man lay near death in the next room.

"Please," I said, pointing at the alcove. "He needs help."

Teresa blinked, her eyes glistening. She glanced in the direction of the alcove and shrugged. "He's supposed to die," she said. "He lied to God and now he has to suffer for his sins."

"Why? What has he done to you?"

"He's the one," she said. "The one who swore on a Bible and sent Paulie to Hell."

It was a strange, disturbing idea, Tim Sullivan sending her husband to Hell with an oath, and it was not until later that I fully understood what she meant. All I knew at that moment was that it was useless to reason with her. At the same time I was aware that Kid Tony could hear every word. Maybe he could be swayed to do the right thing. It didn't seem likely, given his obvious fealty, but it was worth a shot. Reason with Teresa and maybe Tony would respond. What did I have to lose?

"Detective Sullivan didn't have anything to do with your husband's death." I said, eyeing the old fighter. "He's not even with the Metropolitan Police. I think you've got him confused with someone else. Some other policeman."

Teresa looked at me with renewed loathing.

"I know who Lieutenant Detective Timothy Sullivan is," she said. "I know every twitch of his face. On the outside he looks almost normal. On the inside he's one of *them*."

I got the impression that *them* encompassed all of her enemies, real and imagined. Words came pouring out of her, sometimes in disconnected phrases, at other times making a kind of nightmarish sense.

"They came for Paulie," she chattered, her hands tracing shapes in the air. "The itchy things. They came in the windows and down the chimney. I couldn't keep them out, not so many. Then they got inside Paulie's head and made him say bad things, ugly things. What they do, see, they get inside your head and eat your brain," she confided. "Are you listening? Do you understand about *them*?"

"Sure," I nodded.

"Because this is very important, what they do. That's why you can't let them get inside," she confided. "Inside the house, I mean. Once they get inside your head, well, then it's too late. Paulie knew that."

"I'm sure he did," I said, trying to be agreeable. It was a mistake. Teresa caught her breath and pointed at me. Her whole arm quivered. Maybe she thought she was discharging death rays or bolts of mental lightning.

"You knew him," she said. "I tricked you! You knew my Paulie! You're one of *them*."

"I didn't know him," I said. "Honest. I read about him in the newspaper."

There are those who like the print media and those who hate it. Teresa belonged to the latter group. At the word *newspaper* she went berserk. She emitted a low scream that sounded like wind coming through a crack. Flecks of spittle glistened on her lips. Her eyelids fluttered. She ran to the altar, still making that high keening noise, and gathered up a handful of newspaper clippings.

"Lies!" she proclaimed, scattering the clippings over my lap, her movements jittery and manic. "Filthy lies. They say Paulie was a criminal. That's the first lie. There are many, many lies. Criminal? He was a policeman! And because he says nothing, because he will not swear on a Bible and testify against his friends, they decide he must go to jail. Leaving me all alone in that house! I say, 'Paulie, please let me go to jail with you.' But he laughs. Not possible. Not allowed. A wife can't go to jail with her husband. She must remain outside, alone, in a house where the little things that itch the brain come down the chimney and through the windows and out of the faucets. The little itchy things that burrow inside the head, you understand?"

She waited for my reply.

"Yes," I lied. "I understand perfectly."

Her head cocked the other way and again her voice became higher, more girlish. "So he says, Paulie says to Teresa, 'Don't worry, Terry, there's enough money to take care of you. Everything'll be fine.' And Teresa says to Paulie 'Are you nuts? Are you crazy. *I'm* the one who's crazy, remember?' And Paulie, he nods his head. That's all, just nods his head. He knew. *He knew he knew he knew.*"

Teresa beat her fists on the concrete as she chanted the words.

"What did Paulie know?" I asked her.

She turned, striking my legs with her fists. "Knew I couldn't be alone, that's what! Not with the itchy things all around all around, itchy things all around."

The trick, as I saw it, was to try and edit out all the hallucinated garbage she was spewing, the "itchy things" that were burrowing into her mind, and concentrate on the gritty reality. Paulie arrested. Paulie sentenced to jail. The newspaper clippings. Especially the newspapers. She started sorting through the mess of clippings, seizing on particular stories that had become the focus of her rage.

"They had to get him, see?" she said, shoving a Russ White article under my nose. "Had to make Paulie look like the villain. It was all part of the plan. It's a network. They're all infected. They communicate through radio waves. Secret instructions. How to get at Paulie and me. What to say in the papers. All part of the plan. See?" she said, rattling the newsprint. "See the pattern?"

"Ah, maybe if you could explain it," I said uneasily, trying to lean out of range of her furious eyes.

"Explain? You mean you can't see the patterns?"

"It's hard," I said. "Tell me."

The theory here was to ingratiate myself. I'd be her confidant. Then maybe she'd give me back my wheelchair and let me go. That's all I really wanted. Wheels so I could summon help. Wheels so I could get the hell away from mad Teresa before I started believing that Tim Sullivan really was responsible for Paul Cotillo's suicide and all the misery it had caused.

"They said he stole evidence. Drugs. My Paulie!" Teresa laughed. It sounded mechanical, unreal. An impersonation of laughter. "See, the truth is my Paulie *hated* drugs. When his brother would have cocaine, Paulie would get so mad he'd almost cry, *that's* how much he hated drugs. That's why I threw away all my medicine after they tricked him. I knew they'd put poison in the pills. I mean it was *so obvious*. They wanted to drug me so no one would hear the truth."

It was difficult to piece it all together. Was she saying that someone in the Metro police had tried to kill her? Or that she'd stopped taking her medication only after her husband died? I asked her as gently as I knew how, but she didn't respond. Her mind resonated with a one-note threnody and the note was *Paulie, Paulie, Paulie.*

"I told Paulie, I said you've got to concentrate. If you really concentrate they can't get inside your head. But he didn't understand. He couldn't see them coming through the walls. So they got to him. The itchy things. They got inside his head and they made him go in his room and lock the door. They made him pull the trigger. He didn't *want* to do it. He wrote me all about it in the letter."

Going to the altar, she returned with a handwritten note. It was smooth and soft from handling. Reverently she held it out so I could read.

My darling Terry, it began. *Please don't blame yourself for what I am about to do. For a long time I thought I was strong enough to take it but I guess I'm not so strong. Maybe this is what I wanted to do all along, only I was too much of a coward to face it. Now it's the only way out. Your loving husband, Paul.*

Up until that moment I wasn't entirely sure that Paul Cotillo had committed suicide. I thought maybe Teresa, mad as she was, knew something about the circumstances of her husband's death that implicated another cop. The note ended any doubt. Paul Cotillo, facing a long stretch in prison, had scribbled a note to his wife and taken the quickest way out. That was the simple ugly truth that Teresa was unwilling to face.

Knowing that Paul Cotillo had indeed been a suicide didn't really help me. Why did Teresa believe that Tim Sullivan had dispatched her husband to Hell? What could she possibly have against Sully other than the fact that his name had been mentioned in an unrelated newspaper article, and a few scant times on the tube? And why had she gone to the trouble of threatening people involved with a movie that had nothing whatever to do with the sad, unfortunate reality of Paul Cotillo's life?

After putting away the note Teresa wrapped her cool, dry fingers around my wrist and leaned close, whispering, as if she didn't want Kid Tony to overhear. "I'll pay you," she said. "All you have to do is make him die. Antonio won't do this thing for me. But you can. Make him die. Then Paulie can rest in peace."

I had no idea what she was talking about. "You want me to kill Tony?" I whispered, wondering if the big man was paying attention, if he understood.

"No, no, no," she ranted, digging her fingernails into my wrist. "Don't be stupid. Not Tony. Him," she pointed at the alcove where Sully lay. "HIM, HIM, HIM."

I decided it was time to pop the question. Now or never, before her mania reverted into full-blown rage. "But why? I asked. "What did he do to you?"

She stared at me, appalled. How could I be so dense, so stupid? "I told you," she hissed. "He swore on the Bible. He sent Paulie to Hell."

The explanation took hours. I was shown every snapshot tacked to the cross. Paulie's baby pictures. Paulie as a Cub Scout, a Boy Scout, a young, grinning paratrooper. Paulie the day he graduated from the police academy. Paulie with his arm around a gorgeous dark-haired girl with troubled eyes.

"He was a sweet, sweet boy," she said. "None of the other men wanted me, except to do the dirty thing. Paulie was different. So sweet, so kind, so gentle."

And so on. Paul Cotillo was the greatest guy in the world. He was a peach. He held her when she was depressed, took her to doctors and clinics. He sacrificed everything for her: family, career, the prospect of children. Any chance he had of a normal life went down the tubes when he took on Teresa Calvino.

As a rookie cop he'd been ambitious, gung-ho. Swore

he'd make detective before he was thirty. Thirty came and went. He made sergeant, became a petty bureaucrat in Traffic, put in his hours. His real job was at home.

"We lived a secret life, you know? Just me and Paulie. Nobody else. Except sometimes his jerk brother came over, dragged Paulie away to a ball game. Or out with the boys. They had to get their hooks in him somehow! Couldn't stand it he was clean. I heard stuff from the other wives—when they would lower themselves to speak to me, the bitches—I knew their husbands were schemers, thieves. So I said to Paulie, 'Come on, honey, these men you hang out with are scum of the earth. They're dirty cops.' He didn't want to hear it. 'Terry,' he'd say, 'this is my kid brother and his pals you're running down. They like to have a good time is all. They're really a great bunch of guys.' And all the time, all the time this 'great bunch of guys' were scheming. Fixing it so they could keep all the money and Paulie would go to jail."

Teresa believed her husband's participation in the theft of narcotics was part of a conspiracy to ruin her life. If you screened out her paranoid viewpoint it was pretty obvious that the only real conspiracy involved a group of greedy cops who kidded themselves into thinking they could get away with making easy money. When the inevitable happened they had all scrambled to make deals with the prosecution—all but Paul Cotillo, who refused to testify against his younger brother.

"I begged him but he wouldn't listen," Teresa moaned, clutching the photographs to her breast. "He wouldn't listen to me, he'd only listen to them."

"Them?"

She glared at me. "The itchy things. The things that get inside your head and scramble your thoughts. Like I already told you."

So we kept coming back to the imaginary vermin that

invaded the mind. I suppose it was as good a description of madness as any. But I wasn't so sure that Paul Cotillo had been insane when he shot himself. The prospect of doing ten years in Walpole would have been more than a little daunting, especially for an ex-cop.

"Then the detective came," Teresa was saying. "The skinny man with the glasses, Lieutenant Sullivan. I tried to tell him about Paulie, about the itchy things in his head. He pretended to listen but after a while I could tell he was really laughing at me on the inside, no matter how sad he looked on the outside."

This was it, finally. Tim Sullivan's involvement in the Cotillo case. So obvious it had been staring me in the face all along, just as Sheehan taunted when he urged me to leave the investigation to the cops. Sully's involvement with Cotillo had been strictly routine. All deaths by gunshot were investigated by the Homicide Unit, even obvious cases of suicide. Sheehan, with access to the files, had known all along that Sully was the reporting detective for the Cotillo case. And as reporting detective Sully had given testimony at the inquest.

It was that testimony that still burned like a fever in Teresa's mind.

"He put his hand on the Bible and he swore to God that Paulie had shot himself," she said, spitting the words out. "Swore to God! Despondent about his personal life! That's what Detective Sullivan swore. He knew what he was doing. He knew Paulie couldn't get into Heaven after that. *He knew it he knew it he knew it.*"

It was true, in a twisted sort of way. Tim Sullivan, only son of a devout Catholic, would certainly know that suicide was a mortal sin. In the old days suicides were denied burial in consecrated grounds, and still can be denied that blessing if the parish priest has a cold enough heart. The more enlightened view is to allow for the possibility of redemption—that moment of doubt even as the trigger is squeezed—but clearly Teresa was tormented by the belief that her husband's soul was in Hell. A torment augmented by visions and voices.

"I can feel them laughing when I go outside. The laughter comes out of the sewer grates, out of the gutters," she said, covering her ears. "And the lying and the laughing didn't stop after Paulie died. Oh no. There were more lies in the paper about how this same Lieutenant Timothy Sullivan was a hero, a brilliant detective. About how they were making a movie based on his life. The liar! The demon! He sends a man to Hell and he gets a movie! I told the movie people it was all a lie but they wouldn't listen. I'm going to *make* them listen."

There was no point in trying to argue that the Casey movie was about a fictional character based on Sully's career in Homicide. Teresa wouldn't appreciate the distinction. I wasn't sure that I did, for that matter. For me the lives of Sully and Casey were inextricably intertwined. After half-a-dozen novels I was no longer certain precisely where reality left off and fiction began—which is one definition of insanity, or so I've been told.

"Some hero," Teresa said contemptuously. "Does a hero come sneaking around here? Huh? Antonio found him right over there, touching my things on the altar. Touching my things! Putting his terrible fingers all over my Paulie. It wasn't enough he'd killed him and sent him to Hell, he wanted to smear his terrible demon fingers all over Paulie's face!"

So Sully had had the misfortune to stumble into the ruined cellar. That he'd gone in without backup could only mean one thing for a by-the-book cop like Tim Sullivan: he intended it to be an unofficial investigation. He must have suspected all along who'd been making the threatening calls. Must have known who had hired Leland Maddock.

"I think he wanted to help you," I ventured.

It was the wrong thing to say. Teresa's face became a mask of fury.

"Help me!" she raged. "Help me like he helped Paulie? Put me in Hell, *that's* what he meant to do. Well, I fixed him. I picked up the heaviest candlestick and I hit him as hard as I could. Only he wouldn't die. Wasn't that mean? He refused to die. Then I got his gun to shoot him, only he made the bullets disappear."

I glanced at Kid Tony and saw his eyes shift away. My original fix on the old fighter had been close to the mark. Not only was he not responsible for the blow to Sully's head, he'd hidden the bullets from Teresa. And later brought Sully food and water, keeping him alive. Kid Tony was still my best bet, if only I could find a way to appeal to him through Teresa.

"Think about what you're doing," I said to her. "Is this what Paulie wants you to do? Hurt people? Is this what he really wants?"

Teresa shook her head and sighed. I was obviously a major disappointment. "Of course," she said. "Paulie tells me exactly what to do. All you have to do is go up to the altar and listen, really listen, and he'll say the same thing to you."

She grabbed my arms and started tugging. I think she wanted to drag me up to the altar so I could commune with the dead. I'll never know for sure because at that moment a floor timber of the old church creaked. There were distinct footsteps coming from overhead. Someone was up there walking around.

Teresa dropped my arms.

"It's them," she hissed.

CHAPTER TWENTY-FIVE

I DIDN'T EXPECT HER TO SMILE BUT THERE IT was. A big, happy grin. *They* were coming, finally, and for some reason that made her happy. The footsteps quickened—there seemed to be more than one person roaming around up there. Teresa, grinning all the more, ran to the altar. She opened the little door in the fire-blackened tabernacle and removed the empty .38 revolver.

"Don't let her wave that thing around," I warned Kid Tony. "It makes her a target."

He got the idea right away. Getting the gun away from Teresa was a different matter.

"No," she said, dancing away from him. "Pray for bullets. It's the only way to stop them, Antonio. Get down on your knees and pray."

Damaged and broken as he was, Kid Tony still had better moves. He circled as she backed away. When a fist banged against the cellar door she froze, the wild grin fading. He saw his chance and snatched the weapon from her hands.

A voice called from the stairwell: "Anybody down there? Hey Sarge, I heard somethin' move. Better get a light."

Teresa put the candles out. Some of the flames she blew out, others she snuffed with her bare hands.

"Down here!" I shouted. "Hurry!"

Any good cop will draw his weapon when venturing into dark, unknown territory. That's a given. So there was really no one at fault for what happened next. The young plainclothesman who fired blamed himself, of course, but it was over in a heartbeat.

What happened was that the beam of the flashlight found a big, menacing-looking figure crouched with gun in hand, as if taking aim. The cop fired instinctively, hitting Kid Tony square in his heart. A heart that was, I like to think, a pretty big target.

"It was the wheelchair did it," Sheehan said later, after the ambulances had come and gone. "You want to leave a trail behind, a wheelchair is way better than breadcrumbs. I gotta hand it to you, Hawkins, I didn't figure you were that smart. We spot that chair behind the vestry, I knew you had to be nearby."

"She got away," was all I could say.

"Yeah, but you found the lieutenant and we found you. That's what counts."

I should have felt good about it, maybe. I'd come out of it alive. Sully had been rushed to the hospital. Good, fine, but an innocent man was dead and Teresa Cotillo had vanished. Again.

"She had it all planned," Sheehan said. "That's what I think."

He handed me a cigarette. I decided to take up smoking. What the hell.

"She figured that poor bastard would hold the fort," he said. "Which he did, in his own way. There's a little cellar window that exits practically into the bushes. Good cover."

"He saved Sully's life, you know. Hid the bullets. Gave him food and water."

"Yeah, you told me. What a shame." Sheehan shrugged. "Hey, these things happen."

I wondered. Maybe Sheehan was right and Kid Tony had intentionally made himself a target. Maybe that was his way of helping Teresa escape.

"Talk to the priest," I suggested. "He might know where she'd run. I'm pretty sure he knew the cellar was being used as a hideout."

Sheehan nodded. "Yeah, later. Right now he's upset about Torelli. Thinks we shouldn't have gone in like we did. I tell him, I say, come on, Father, the pair of 'em had a cop as hostage, not to mention a dumb civilian can't mind his own business. What'd you expect us to do, wait for an invite? I tell him, hey, you want to blame somebody, blame that crazy broad—she's the one got Kid Tony killed. Know what the guy does, this skinny guinea priest? He tries to pop me one! Can you beat it? Like I insulted his girlfriend or his mother."

Or maybe a little of each. The girlfriend he'd never had, the mother he hadn't been able to help. Or maybe it wasn't like that at all. The priest was just part of the mixed-up, shook-up world Sully had stumbled into. It yielded no easy answers, no pat solutions.

"We'll get her," Sheehan said, grinding a cigarette under his skiny black shoes. "Matter of time."

They were fools. It took so little to fool them. In a dumpster she had found a tattered yellow plastic raincoat and hat. She put them on, stood at a bus stop, and became invisible. A cop car went right by the bus stop, slowing down, and she smiled and waved. The cop inside, a young kid, smiled and waved back.

Fools. The itchy things made them slow and stupid.

It was going to be easy to trick them. And this time she would do it alone.

Later, in the elevator at Mass General Hospital, Larry Sheehan showed a lot less confidence.

Sully had been in surgery for hours—something about relieving pressure on his brain. Sheehan, always cat nervous in hospital situations, had worn the shine off the lobby floor, pacing as we waited for the news. When the surgeon called the desk Sheehan grabbed the phone. I watched the color drain from his face as he listened.

The Chelsea tough guy started losing it as the elevator slowly ascended to the third floor CICU, where Sully had been transferred after surgery.

"He might as well be dead, Jack," he said. Tears poured down his pallid, scrawny cheeks. "She cracked his skull like a goddamn walnut."

"He's alive," I said.

"Yeah," Sheehan muttered. "Right. The doc wouldn't come right out and say it but I got the impression the lieutenant's in a coma."

For security puposes Sully had been shuttled into a cardiac intensive care unit. Leaving the elevator banks we followed colored stripes through a maze of corridors. I concentrated on bricking up the dam in my head that held back a flood of traumatic memories associated with my long stay in this very same hospital. Months of anxious waiting. Waiting for doctor, waiting for nurse. Waiting for the numbness below my hips to recede. It never happened.

The colored stripes brought us to an unmarked door. In the corridor a black custodian mopped furtively, as if concerned that the soapy water might damage his Air Jordans.

"No guard?" I asked.

Sheehan gave me a look. "Relax. If I wasn't with you, Hank woulda already blown a hole in your tire. Right Hank?"

The undercover detective with the mop smiled and said, "Absolutely, Sergeant."

Two more detectives were on station just inside the CICU, dressed in orderly greens. There were twelve patients in the unit. Several were on postsurgical ventilators and the clunk-hiss-clunk of mechanized breathing made me feel like I'd swallowed a snowball.

"There he is," Sheehan whispered.

Sully was plainly down for the count. He was connected to monitoring devices and his heavily bandaged head was supported by a complicated rubber brace. He was breathing on his own, at least. Both of his eyes were swollen shut and his left cheekbone was badly bruised.

The nurse assigned to him seemed no more than a girl, although a brief conversation convinced me she was competent.

"He's in a coma, right?" Sheehan asked her right off.

She shook her head. "No way," she said. "Coma is a pejorative term. At this point it would be more helpful to think of your friend as deeply asleep. He has a fractured skull and there has been trauma and swelling in the frontal tissue. Deep sleep is exactly what he needs while his brain sorts out the damage."

I said, "So he's not brain dead?"

"Absolutely not. We're getting deep alpha rhythms but the waves aren't flat. No way. He's alive in there."

I began to have the same problem Sheehan had in the elevator. The nurse handed me a tissue. I got the impression they handed out a lot of tissues in the CICU.

Sheehan remained there to coordinate security. Outside in the hall Hank the supposed custodian wanted a word.

"They got a line on the perp yet?" he asked.

"*You're* asking *me*?"

"Man, I'm on the guard detail, you dig?" he said, leaning on the mop. "Don't tell us nothing. Thought you might know something since you tight with the sergeant."

I chuckled. "Don't say that to Larry."

"See? You call him Larry. Me, I never dream of that. Uh-uh. Sergeant Detective Sheehan, *sir*. He ever make lieutenant we all gonna have to kiss his pinkie ring."

I thought for a moment. "He doesn't have a pinkie ring."

Hank grinned. "See? You tight with the man. You know."

Tight with Larry Sheehan, the Chelsea tough guy. What a mind-boggling idea.

Megan had an opinion about my activities in the North End.

"You dumb bastard," she said. "That's the stupidest thing you've ever done."

"Hey, all I did was go talk to a priest. The rest was accidental. Besides, if I hadn't checked out that cellar Sully'd still be down there."

That wasn't entirely correct. An APB for Kid Tony had been issued earlier in the day. Sheehan's undercover squad had been conducting a building-by-building search of the area when they spotted my wheelchair. So the professionals were on a collision course with Torelli even before I stumbled—or rather rolled—into the situation.

Meg calmed down when I described Sully's condition.

"Is he going to make it?" she wanted to know.

"The prognosis is guarded. They assume he'll survive the head trauma. What they're worried about is brain damage. Which they can't really check out until he's fully conscious."

Meg said, "He'll be fine. I've got this feeling."

Megan's intuition is an iffy thing. Sometimes it's right on, witness her original attraction to yours truly. Other times she's way off—for instance the one and only time we went to Rockingham Park and she blew a cool grand on a knock-kneed longshot that never did get all the way around the track.

"I know what you're thinking," she said. "You'll never let me forget it, will you? One lousy horse."

"Intuition," I said.

"Hey, what can I say? With me it works for people, not horses."

It was one of those weird funerals with no coffin. Kid Tony's body would not be released for burial until the investigation of the shooting was complete. Given the speed with which the Internal Affairs boys proceeded, that might be months, or even years. Father Fabrizzi decided to go ahead with the Mass, body or no body.

"The mortal remains are insignificant," he explained before the service began. "Antonio's soul is already with God. I believe that."

Faith in the life everlasting didn't afford the priest much comfort, apparently. When Meg and I found him in the rectory garden his eyes were wet. He clasped the breviary to his chest but it didn't help much. His hands were still shaking.

"The police said they might arrest me," he said. "They kill Antonio and now they want to arrest me. It's absurd."

"They mention any charges?"

He nodded. "Accessory to kidnapping."

"Tell me, Father, did you know they were holding Lieutenant Sullivan?"

"No. Of course not."

"Tell you what, after the service I'll introduce you to a good lawyer."

The funeral was not largely attended. There was Russ White, doing the obligatory while he followed up his story. Megan, myself, and Fitzy. A few shifty-eyed specimens who could have been sportswriters or process servers, a professional mourner, famous in certain circles, who worked for Fat Lenny Calvino, and the rectory housekeeper. There were also three undercover detectives covering the exits and the empty organ loft.

"Why the stooges?" Fitzy wanted to know.

"In case Teresa decides to drop in," I whispered.

The Mass was conducted in Italian. There was no sermon. Father Fabrizzi seemed in a hurry to get it over with. Maybe the presence of police officers made him nervous, or it could have been Fat Lenny's mourner, who felt obliged to weep copiously.

"That ghoul can turn it on like a faucet," Meg observed.

"He's had plenty of practice."

I kept an eye on the organ loft. If I'd been writing a Casey story that's where the villain would have appeared. Equipped with a high-powered rifle or maybe, just for effect, one of General Gritz's plastic machine pistols. I'd have Casey throw off her aim by striking a chord on the organ—a nice touch. Something from Verdi's *Requiem*, a favorite of Casey's. And mine, for that matter.

There would be no requiem for this particular heavyweight, though. In death as in life Kid Tony got the small-potato treatment. A quick service and out the door. No eulogy. No Teresa.

"Just what I need," Fitzy complained when I suggested he speak to Father Fabrizzi. "A client who's taken a vow of poverty."

"He's right up your alley," I assured him. "Fat Lenny hates him, the Boston Police are trying to bust him, and the archbishop wants him on the next boat back to Naples."

Fitzy perked right up. He loves an underdog.

"The bastards," he said. "We'll sue."

The transformation was complete. No one would ever recognize her now. The old Teresa was gone. The new Teresa was in place. Ready and waiting for an opportunity to make him die.

"Revenge is mine, sayeth the Lord," she prayed.

"What's that honey? You talking to me?"

"Just talking to myself," the new Teresa said gaily.

"No harm in that," the older woman said. "Get's so crazy in here you can't help but talk to yourself sometime. You new on this shift, honey?"

"Filling in," the new Teresa said. "I'm just filling in."

Inside the old Teresa waited. Crouching in the imagined darkness.

Waiting to come screaming into the light.

CHAPTER TWENTY-SIX

IT WAS THE PERFECT SETTING FOR A MURDER. A place where beautiful people posed and laughed and traded lies and sipped champagne. Where guitars gently wept and the social vampires flashed bloodless smiles and everybody's hair was perfect.

The wrap party. Dinner at Henry's Harborside for the cast, crew, and various groupies associated with the production of *Casey and the Blond Widow* in the elegant glass-walled banquet room that overlooks the inner harbor and the city skyline. The room with the teak floors and the crystal chandeliers and that game they play with the live lobsters.

It goes like this: the lobsters crawl around a big glass tank, each with a bright yellow number affixed to one claw, and you pick a number and Henry's beautiful waiters scoop your dinner from the tank and then bring you the steaming lobster on a big plate and the yellow number on a small plate, and it's true, at Henry's Harborside you can have your crustacean and eat it, too.

Megan said, "Pass the butter, my love."

"My love?"

"Seafood does it to me," she said in a low, husky voice. "That and being in close proximity to Burt Bardo."

"Are you serious?"

"What can I say? He's a hunk. First movie star that ever gave me the tingles was Sean Connery. The second was Burt Bardo. That remake of *The Gunfighter*."

"Too bad," I said. "I kind of liked the guy until you said that. Tingles? What do you mean by tingles, exactly?"

Meg smirked and batted her eyelashes. She was teasing, getting back at me for not putting up a fight when Lindy Bangs tried to lick my tonsils earlier in the evening. And I wasn't worried about Bardo, not really. He had a distant look in his eye that convinced me he'd just as soon be elsewhere. He poked at his lobster without much enthusiasm. No tingles for Burt, not tonight.

"He looks lonesome," Meg observed.

"His next movie's in turnaround," I said knowingly.

"Speak English."

"He's out of work."

Meg shrugged. Clearly she didn't think a hunk like Bardo would be out of work for long. "The *Globe* ran a feature on him today. He sure takes a nice picture."

"Give it a rest," I said.

Clarence Higgs decided to drop by our table for a chat. He nearly missed the chair. Didn't spill a drop of his champagne, though. He was glassy eyed and his nose looked parboiled. "Hear about break in?" he wanted to know. Remarkably his speech wasn't slurred, although he had an odd habit of leaving out certain words.

"Break in?"

"Property trailer," he said. "Bloody disgrace. Hire security guard, the son bitch falls asleep! Busted lock, see? Trashed place. Torn it apart."

"You reported it?"

"Damn right. Insurance. Got to file." He nodded slowly, breathing heavily through his nose. "Ripped off costumes, props. Spray paint all over. Disgusting mess."

"Sounds like a gang of kids."

He shrugged. The gesture was so exaggerated he lost his balance and almost fell out of the chair. After recovering he mumbled, "Kids? Maybe. Maybe not. Spray paint, see?"

"I get it," I said. "Graffiti. Had to be kids."

Higgs shook his head. His eyes were bulging. I realized it was more than alcohol that was bothering him. He was anxious because one of the equipment trailers had been trashed. I didn't understand what the big deal was, or why he was telling me about it, and said so.

"Black paint," he said. "One word over and over. Dead." He held up his hand and pretended to spray paint the letters. "D-E-A-D. Dead."

I'd had a few glasses of champagne myself, which may explain why it took a while for the message to get through. Clarence was informing me that the movie company had been robbed by someone who left a curious message behind.

"Could be her," he said, staring sadly at his empty glass. "That's what cops said."

"Who?" Meg said, breaking in. "What's he talking about?"

"It's possible Teresa broke into one of the storage trailers and took some stuff, right Clarence?"

He nodded. "Dead," he said. "Short, sweet."

"What did she steal, Clarence, do you know?"

"Props," he said. "Costume stuff. Inventory tomorrow."

I suddenly felt a very pressing need to get to a telephone. Megan followed me out to the lobby. "I get it," she said. "This is a ploy to get me away from Burt Bardo. You're afraid I might swoon into his arms."

"Got two bits?"

She made a face and handed me a quarter. Running down Larry Sheehan was easier than I expected. I called the Turret and they transferred me to a secure line at the hospital, where he was heading up the guard detail.

"Make it snappy," Sheehan growled. "I'm puttin' moves on one a the nurses. Cute little blond with big blue eyes."

I relayed Clarence Higgs's information about the property trailer being ransacked.

"Yeah, I heard about that," Sheehan said. "We put men in the area but she was long gone."

"You sure it was Teresa?"

"Ninety percent. She told you she was going after the movie company, right? Looks like she did. Left a couple of burnt-out candles in the trailer, I sent the wax drippings over to Forensic to see if they can be matched to the candles in the cellar. What I'm saying, Hawkins, as usual we got it covered."

"Right," I said. "So how's Sully?"

"Okay, I guess. Sat up for a while. He's talking pretty normal. Still don't remember nothing after he left the house that morning. Doc says he might never recover that memory. Traumatic amnesia, they call it."

"Yeah. Listen, the reason I'm bothering you, I've got this hunch about what Teresa was doing in that trailer."

Sheehan chuckled. "Hey, you ain't even seen the place and you got a hunch? What is this? I'll tell you what that crazy broad was doing. She was going berserk in there. She tore it all apart and then she painted it black. It don't make sense. Nothing this broad does makes sense."

"Maybe," I said. "Except she picked a pretty specific target."

"A goddam trailer? That's specific?"

"It's a property trailer, Larry."

"So what. Property of the movie company, big deal."

"Costumes, Larry. There's more than one property trailer. The one she hit had props and costumes. All kinds of costumes. Wigs, uniforms."

I could hear Sheehan exhaling slowly. "Jesus Christ," he said. "What kind of uniforms?"

"All kinds," I said. "Cop uniforms. Doctor outfits. Nurse outfits."

I had trouble concentrating on all the fun I was supposed to be having. The wrap party was in full swing when we returned to the table. A DJ with spiked hair was pumping Top Forty tunes through a set of booming speakers. Lindy Bangs threw herself into the dance with abandon, her little black mini flouncing around her hips. Ordinarily the sight would have cheered me. As it was I kept thinking about Teresa prowling the corridors of the hospital.

D-E-A-D.

As Clarence Higgs had said, it was short and sweet. Very much to the point. It convinced me that Teresa, having run out of helpers, intended to finish the job herself.

"Don't worry," Meg said, squeezing my hand. "It's a great big hospital. Five buildings, a dozen floors. Sully's registered under an assumed name with cardiac patients, so she'll never be able to locate his room."

"You're probably right."

"No 'probably', Jack. And even if she does find out

where Sully is, Sheehan's ready for her. Leland Maddock couldn't get through Larry Sheehan and he was a professional killer."

"Teresa's an unpredictable lady," I said. "You never know what she'll do."

You never know. I had that part of it right.

Burt Bardo hobbled off the dance floor and collapsed into a chair next to Megan. "This is what happens when you get middle aged," he panted. "Sexy young directors stab you with stiletto heels, then leave you to fend for yourself."

His expensive hairpiece was slightly askew. He caught me looking, grinned, and fixed it with a deft touch of his fingertips. "Cocktail waitress been around?" he asked. "I could use a drink."

Lindy came off the floor holding a broken heel. She perched next to Bardo and gave him a kiss on the cheek. "Sorry love. Will you live?"

"If I get a drink, yeah."

Lindy ignored him and turned to Meg. "Megan darling. Did I tell you about me and Richard Random? No? Oh, God, I'm so excited! I'm going to *direct* him, can you believe it?"

I noticed Bardo wince when he heard the name. Obviously he wasn't a fan of Richard Random. Whoever Richard Random was.

"I almost fainted when they told me," Lindy was saying. "I never watch the daytime soaps. Well, almost never. Except for 'Naked Village' of course. *Everyone* watches 'Naked Village.'"

I felt out of it. I'd never heard of "Naked Village." It was, Lindy said, a hot new serial drama set in a place a lot like the Malibu colony. Celebrities and surfers in various combinations. Richard Random played a surfer.

From what Lindy said most of his surfing was done on silk sheets.

"The network wants to try him out on prime time. And I got the call. Isn't that fabulous?"

We all agreed it was fabulous. Burt Bardo raised his hand and signaled for a waitress. If I read his expression correctly he was thinking that Richard Random wouldn't have to wave his arms to attract attention.

"I can't wait to get back to the coast," Lindy said. "I mean Boston, it's okay, but the *weather*. Spare me. Right, Burt?"

He shrugged. "You're the director. I'm just an out-of-work actor."

Lindy giggled. "Isn't he awful? They're all the same, actors. No matter how successful they are, how popular they get, they're always afraid they'll never work again. It's like a virus or something."

"Exactly," Bardo said grumpily. "Now where's my medication?"

I knew there was something odd about the cocktail waitress who finally arrived with Bardo's drink, but I couldn't put my finger on it. Partly it was her thick blond hair, I decided. It was just too blond and too thick. Then there was her awkwardness with the tray. Nervous about waiting on a celebrity, maybe. And then there was the purse. Since when did a Harborside cocktail waitress carry a purse to the tables?

The explanation dawned on me just as Burt Bardo reached for his drink, but by then things were already in motion:

The tray was falling.

The cocktail waitress was reaching into her purse. Pulling out a knife with a long silvery blade.

Bardo had the drink to his lips when he glimpsed the knife descending and tried to shove himself back.

Too late.

Megan reached out and grabbed at the waitress, yanking her hair.

Too late.

The knife plunged into Bardo's chest. A red crescent bloomed over his heart. He looked down, dumbfounded.

That's when it got very confusing. I remember Megan beating at Teresa with the blond wig. I remember several people, Clarence Higgs among them, wrestling her to the floor and taking the knife away. I remember Bardo looking at the red stain over his heart and saying, "Just my luck," before he passed out.

He was pretty sanguine about it, considering he'd been knifed in the heart. While we were waiting for the cops to arrive Bardo giggled and said, "Hey, maybe it'll help the ratings. Whattaya think, Lindy? Anybody stabbed Richard Random lately?"

"How can you laugh?" she responded, fussing over him with a moistened hankie. It was a nice try, but the shirt was ruined. "I thought you were killed. Dead."

It was a matter of props. Prop wig, prop knife. Retracting blade, stage blood in the handle. Very convincing to us amateurs. Very convincing to Burt Bardo for a few moments.

"Get me out of this crazy town," Lindy said, stealing a sip from his drink. "Get me back to good old normal Lala Land."

The DJ was blasting tunes to an empty dance floor. Just about everybody had boogied to the bar. Seeking to calm the jitters and discuss the event. The rumor, instantly formed, was that the attack was staged, part of a publicity stunt.

"You suppose she thought the knife was real?" Meg wanted to know.

"Haven't a clue," I said. "You'll have to ask Teresa."

We never got the chance. It didn't take long for the squad cars to converge on the restaurant. By then Teresa was out of it. She lay on her side, knees up to her chin. Her eyes fluttered white. Her mouth was open wide, as if she were screaming. Except there wasn't a peep out of her. A silent scream. A rare manifestation, the experts tell me, of catatonia. She held that terrible pose as they strapped her to the gurney and took her away. Russ White told me she was still doing it when they brought her up for arraignment and ordered her committed for observation.

That was a year ago. As far as I know she's still screaming.

EPILOGUE

CRAZY MAY NOT BE CATCHING, BUT IT'S EASY to pick up the symptoms. For instance I went nuts when *Casey and the Blond Widow* was broadcast on a damp, dreary night in early December.

Fitzy played host. He rented a big screen for the evening, handled the invitations, such as they were. Most of the people I really cared about were there. Lois and the twins, of course. Mary Kean, my editor. Russ White and his current flame. Sully showed up late and left early— he was still a little shaky then, and anyhow he hates movies. Larry Sheehan stayed to the bitter end, though, and laughed the loudest.

Megan never giggled. Not once, bless her.

It started out fine. Lois passed trays of finger food. Fitzy played bartender while Sheehan, who had just come off duty, entertained us with the latest developments in the continuing saga of General George Gritz.

"What happened is the grand jury finally got a star witness," Sheehan explained. "Big secret, right? The DA has been trying to get a felony indictment for months, but contrary to what usually happens, the good citizens in the jury weren't cooperating. The trouble is that Gritz has been up to testify two, three times, right? Each time he gets more charming. The jurors think he's an American patriot. The more he waves the flag, the more they love him."

"He's the P. T. Barnum of Murder, Incorporated," Fitzy agreed. "I'll bet his motto is 'There's a sucker killed every minute.'"

"Yeah, well they finally cooked his goose," Sheehan said knowingly. "The indictments came down today."

"That so? How'd they turn the jury?"

"Like I said, a secret witness. Any guesses? No? I'll give you a hint. He looks like a basset hound."

"Captain Beaker?!"

"On the button, Russ. It seems that Captain Beaker, the general's head honcho, was an FBI plant. Had him undercover with the general for five years. The way I heard it, when Beaker and Gritz passed in the hall outside the grand jury room, the general tried to beat him with that cane he carries ever since he shot his toe off. Took three officers of the court to restrain him. So Beaker goes in there with that long nose of his bleeding and tells the jury that yes indeed, the general was well aware that *American Mercenary* was being used to facilitate contact with killers-for-hire."

"I don't get it," Meg said. "Why would a multimillionaire do a thing like that? Not for the money, surely."

Sheehan squinted into his beer bottle, avoiding eye contact. Typical Sheehan behavior while in the presence of an attractive woman. He mumbled, "According to Beaker's testimony, Gritz considered it the ultimate freedom of expression. The right to express your desire to kill people for money."

"So it's his word against the general's?"

"Not quite," Sheehan said. "Beaker was wired. They got about two years' worth of Gritz mouthing off on tape."

"Does that mean he'll go to jail?"

Sheehan was scornful. "Gimme a break. You said it, right? The guy's super rich. If you know anything about the so-called criminal justice system you know the rich don't do time."

"Tut-tut," Fitzy said, wagging his finger. "I figure Gritz'll get three to five."

"No way," Sheehan said.

"Not in jail, maybe," Fitzy said. "But years in court, which is the next best thing. No matter what happens with the felony charges, the civil suits will keep coming. Old give-em-hell George is going to be a professional defendant, mark my words."

"Lawyers," Sheehan said, as if pronouncing a disease.

For once I kept my mouth shut, avoiding the inevitable cops-and-shysters argument that erupts whenever Fitzy and Sheehan occupy the same room. I concentrated on trying to act cool about the television premiere of Casey. Tried and failed. My creation, right there on the boob tube! Damn, but it was exciting. So what if they had trashed my script, changed the title, altered the plot? Casey was still mine, right?

Wrong.

We found out just how wrong when Fitzy dimmed the lights at the appointed hour. Mary Kean bussed me on the cheek as the title sequence rolled. Megan tightened her grip on my hand. And within two minutes a plague of laughter descended from the airwaves.

215

"Hey, this is weird," Sheehan said. "This ain't what I expected."

My Casey story, a tale of nail-biting suspense, had been reedited into a comedy. A farce. Complete with canned laughter. Which would have been okay, I guess, if there had been any real humor in it. I mean I can take a joke as well as the next guy, if you give me a chance. But the movie hadn't been conceived as a comedy, nor was it shot for intentional comic effect. What happened was the network, having deemed the first effort unsatisfactory, had exercised an option to recut it, stringing together all the blown takes. Burt Bardo tripping over his lines, bumping into doors, dropping his gun. The usual celluloid detritus that's supposed to end up on the cutting room floor. Instead of intrigue and suspense we got ninety excruciating minutes of Casey as a nitwit detective, incapable of solving a crime.

"What a riot," Sheehan said when the last pathetic scene concluded. "I got a kick out of it when his toupee blew off. I had no idea Burt Bardo was such a funny guy."

"Neither did he," I sighed. "Neither did he."

It was a bad news, good news month. The bad news was the movie. The good news happened Christmas Eve, on Nantucket. There are a lot of lovely inns on the island. Meg chose the Metcalf because it overlooks the harbor and because the proprietor happens to be a justice of the peace. We asked for the short ceremony, and got it.

Megan said, "I do."

I said, "I'd be a fool not to. Yes. You bet."

Megan said, "Just a plain 'I do' would have been sufficient."

I said, "Don't edit me, please."

So we drank too much champagne and watched the snowflakes melt against the window panes and recited poetry and did a lot of other silly things. It was exhausting, being so happy. Eventually we fell asleep. I was fully prepared to sleep until the New Year, at least, but the telephone started to ring just before dawn.

It rang for a good long while.

"Shoot it," Meg said.

"Can't," I said. "Out of ammo."

"Then answer it."

I picked up the phone. Someone on the other end was crying or laughing, I couldn't tell which. Whoever it was insisted on speaking to Megan.

"Tell 'em to go to hell," Meg said when I pried the pillow away from her head.

"Tried that," I said.

Meg took the call, of course. When she sat up the covers slipped down to her hips. I was admiring the effect when she put her hand over the receiver and gave me a funny look.

"It's Lindy Bangs," she said. "I think she just killed Richard Random."